First baby of the new ... Flying D

Brice seemed bigger holding her tiny daughter, looking awkward and awed all at the same time.

Madison smiled and held out her hand.

He moved forward carefully, leaned down and placed the baby in her arms.

Brice was so strikingly...*male.* Surely it was the flood of extra childbirth hormones that caused her to catch her breath at the sight of him. She'd seen cowboys before, but mostly the spiffed-up kind in Dallas. This man was a working cowboy. The kind of man who spent most of his life in the saddle. And he made her feel safe, secure....

"Everything appears to be there," Brice said.

"Thank you, Brice. For my daughter."

He shrugged. "All in a day's work."

Somehow Madison didn't think so. Amazing how a handful of baby could cause a tough man like Brice to sweat—and to smile.

Books by Mindy Neff

HARLEQUIN AMERICAN ROMANCE

*Texas Sweethearts

Don't miss any of our special offers. Write to us at the following address for information on our newest releases.

Harlequin Reader Service
U.S.: 3010 Walden Ave., P.O. Box 1325, Buffalo, NY 14269
Canadian: P.O. Box 609, Fort Erie, Ont. L2A 5X3

The Cowboy Is a Daddy

Mindy Neff

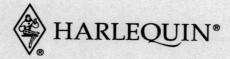

TORONTO • NEW YORK • LONDON
AMSTERDAM • PARIS • SYDNEY • HAMBURG
STOCKHOLM • ATHENS • TOKYO • MILAN • MADRID
PRAGUE • WARSAW • BUDAPEST • AUCKLAND

Recycling programs
for this product may
not exist in your area.

ISBN-13: 978-0-373-36333-9

THE COWBOY IS A DADDY

ABOUT THE AUTHOR

Mindy Neff published her first book with Harlequin American Romance in 1995. Since then, she has appeared regularly on the Waldenbooks bestseller list and won numerous awards, including a National Readers' Choice award, an *RT Book Reviews* Career Achievement award and three W.I.S.H. awards for outstanding hero, and has been nominated twice for the prestigious RITA® Award.

Originally from Louisiana, Mindy settled in Southern California, where she married a really romantic guy and raised five kids. Family, friends, reading, grandkids and a very spoiled Maltese named Harley are her passions.

Chapter One

They called him "BAD" DeWitt. And it wasn't just his initials that had earned him the reputation in four counties of Wyoming.

For a while, after his wife had left, Brice had gone out of his way to raise hell. He'd drunk too much, caroused more than he cared to remember and earned himself a healthy amount of respect over the use of his fists—not to mention the dent in his checkbook over paying for busted-up bar furniture.

Well, those days were behind him now; time had a way of healing wounds.

Or so he thought. An uneasy feeling nagged at him tonight, a sense of expectancy shimmering in the crisp night air that slid in through the partially opened window. He stood in the middle of the living room, trying to shake the prickling sensation, listening to the familiar sounds of the ranch. A coyote bayed in the distance, disturbing the horses. From the barn, Samson nickered then settled down. The low of cows carried across the prairie, and Brice wondered if he should get the twelve-gauge and ride out to check on the herd, just to make sure some hungry critter wasn't eyeing his heifers as a midnight snack.

He made it as far as the window, barely noticing the near-freezing wind that whistled through the slight opening at the bottom. It was below ten degrees out, but that didn't matter to Brice. He always left at least one of the windows or doors cracked, a habit he'd developed after being trapped in a well as a kid—the very day his mom had run off, making his dark, prisonlike terror a lasting nightmare because nobody had been around to look for him.

He shook away the memory.

Behind him, the TV, via state-of-the-art satellite dish, belted out sounds of revelers on one of the traditional New Year's Eve broadcasts.

Brice looked at the clock. It was one hour to midnight. One hour to the beginning of the new year.

And here he stood, alone in his living room, with only the sound of television partyers—strangers—to keep him company, telling himself that he was *not* lonely.

Hell, the guys had asked him to come down to the bunkhouse to ring in the new year, but he'd declined. There was even a message on the machine from Janie Perkins inviting him to drive to the city.

But he just hadn't been in the mood to socialize. Rubbing the back of his neck, he glanced again at the Waltham mantel clock, wondering what the new year would bring.

Hopefully a housekeeper and cook. Moe had threatened to quit three times in the past week, usually after Brice had burned the flapjacks or forgotten to start the coffee. Oh, he knew how to cook, it's just that it had been a while since he'd had to do it, and he was rusty.

And he flat-out didn't have the time. As it was, he'd been burning the candle at both ends ever since his housekeeper, Lavina, had gone off to care for her daughter and grandkids, leaving him with a three-thousand-square-foot ranch house and eight hard-working cowboys to feed.

And since then only one woman had answered his ad for the housekeeper-cook position—a woman by the name of Madison Carlyle. He hoped she wasn't so old that she couldn't handle the heavy duties.

On the other hand he hoped she would just show up. He'd expected her two days ago and had lost precious hours hanging around waiting.

He couldn't keep sending Moe out to ride ramrod in search of stray cattle or to keep the troughs from icing over. Moe was getting too old for these cold-weather conditions, even though the stubborn cuss wouldn't admit that his rheumatism was darned near crippling him.

The revelers on the television were starting to annoy Brice. A man could only take so much screaming and yelling and happiness, especially a man who was used to and appreciated silence. But just as he headed across the room to shut off the program, the doorbell pealed.

Ah, hell. Surely Janie hadn't made the two-hour drive from the city just because he hadn't returned her phone call. He liked Janie well enough, but there was something missing between them. Besides, Janie Perkins was a city girl through and through, and Brice had learned his lesson well in that regard.

Steer clear.

Prepared to be polite but firm, he pulled open the door, a cold gust of wind sucking out the heat. The woman who stood shivering on the porch was tiny—all bundled up in a fancy coat with some fussy fur around the hooded collar.

Definitely a city gal and definitely not Janie.

For a minute all he could do was stare, feeling as though he'd been kicked in the gut by an angry mustang. Her face was china-doll smooth and glowing with good health. She wasn't beautiful, but there was something about those clear blue eyes that nearly knocked him senseless.

"Your car break down?" he asked when he finally found his voice. With only eight families living along a fifty-mile stretch of road, strangers happening by wasn't a common occurrence. Then he glanced down at the oversize, cloth suitcase at her feet, its handle still extended, its wheels resting drunkenly half on and half off the top porch step.

"As a matter of fact it did," she said in a rush. She tucked a strand of golden hair back into her fur-lined hood. "First, I got lost—I didn't think that was possible with all this flat land—then, when I gained my bearings, the car quit on me. I'm Madison Carlyle, by the way, the new housekeeper." She shivered and pulled her inadequate coat more tightly around her. "Is your father home?"

He felt his hairline shift in surprise. "He died about five years back."

"Oh! Oh, I'm sorry. I'd expected someone older. Are you Mr. DeWitt, then?"

"Brice." He still felt poleaxed and couldn't stop himself from staring. She had a light, musical voice that made his blood sing. The fact that she assumed he was young played right into his battered male ego. Sometimes he felt more like eighty-two rather than thirty-two.

"Well, thank goodness I've got the right ranch. I stopped in a little town about forty-five minutes back, and a gentleman at the filling station gave me directions."

"That was probably Leonard. He's the town mechanic. Didn't you ask him about your car?"

"There wasn't any need. It was running fine then. The darn thing only decided to act up a mile or so back." She rubbed the small of her back and gave him a tentative smile. "I know it's an ungodly hour to show up for work, but…can I come in?"

"Sorry." Hell, DeWitt, your manners stink. He grabbed her suitcase, then stepped back as she entered and shut the door behind her. "Here, let me take your coat."

She tightened her hold on the furry lapels. "I'm a little cold at the moment."

He frowned at the hesitation and evasion. "And so's your coat. You'll warm up faster by the fire."

Something in her soft blue eyes telegraphed reluctance—or guilt? But at last she sighed and released her death grip on the thin, wool material. Removing her gloves, she slipped the oversize coat buttons through their loops.

If he'd been staring—and admiring before—now his eyes went even wider when he finally registered what he was actually seeing. Beneath her fuzzy red smock, her belly was the size of a watermelon.

At a total loss for words, Brice realized that his one and only applicant—whom he'd hired sight unseen—was pregnant as all get-out.

Ah, hell. True, she wasn't elderly as he'd feared, but she was definitely pregnant. And aside from her condition, she was no bigger than a minute. He needed somebody who could cook for his ranch hands and see to the house. With the weather threatening to turn nasty, the last thing he needed was worries over being snowed in with a woman in labor. He already had enough on his plate, thank you very much.

But he couldn't toss her back out the door at eleven o'clock at night. And it was too dark to check out her vehicle tonight.

She massaged her back and held his gaze, those eyes of hers hinting at vulnerability—yet her stubborn chin jutted out as though inviting him to find fault. He had an idea this little lady would give as good as she got.

Still, his words wouldn't be silenced. "Seems you forgot to mention something on your application." He glanced at her belly, then for some dang reason, felt shy at doing so. "You also didn't mention there being a *Mr.* Carlyle."

"There isn't one."

"Just a baby Carlyle." Divorced? he wondered. He gazed at her finger, didn't see a ring.

"Look, Mr. DeWitt—"

"Brice."

"Brice, then. I need a job. And I assure you, I can—" Her eyes widened and her breath hitched on a gasp as she doubled over. "Oooh."

Forgetting about absentee husbands and wedding rings, Brice dropped her coat right there in the entry hall and hovered, his heart slamming against his ribs in a surge of adrenaline brought on by pure masculine panic.

"What?" He didn't mean to shout. "What's wrong?"

"Um…" She took a deep breath, her cheeks darkening with a flush. "I think my water just broke."

"Your…?" He glanced down, saw the dampness on her stretch pants, saw the moisture on the floor. "Holy cow!" His gaze lifted from her bulging stomach—to the indignant frown lines created by her tightly drawn blond brows. "Er, not you! I wasn't calling you…I meant…ah, hell, sit down somewhere." He felt totally out of control. Damn it, he *was* out of control. And the fool woman was actually smiling at him. A little trembly, but a smile nonetheless.

"I'm fine—I think," she said.

"Not according to that puddle of water at your feet—" His words broke off as she moaned and bent double again. "Oh, man, tell me what to do." He hovered some more, but she waved him back, breathing deeply.

After less than a minute she straightened. "That was a rough one."

"Is it done?"

She nodded.

Thank you, God. "Okay, uh, maybe you better sit down somewhere. Anywhere. I'll call…" Who, damn it? "Well, you sit. I'll call." *Somebody!* At the moment not a soul came to mind. Man, he was a mess. Heck of a New Year's Eve. He was so flustered that in spite of his ridiculous command for her to sit, he swooped her into his arms and carried her to the sofa.

"No! I'll ruin your furniture."

"Right now I don't care squat about the furniture." But he changed directions and headed toward the bedroom. Women in labor were supposed to be in a bed, weren't they?

"I'm sorry to be such a nuisance. This wasn't supposed to happen. I'm not due for another three weeks."

That gave him a little hope, yet the eerie sense of expectancy he'd felt earlier returned full force. "So maybe this isn't the real thing?"

"That's what I told myself this morning."

He came to an abrupt halt just inside his bedroom and nearly dropped her. "This morning!"

"Being in pain doesn't make me deaf," she admonished.

He made an effort to stay calm. "If you were in labor this morning, why did you keep driving?"

"I thought it was just Braxton Hicks contractions."

"Braxton..."

"False labor."

"Could it still be?"

She shook her head, her silky blond hair tickling his chin. "'Fraid not. How close is the nearest hospital?"

"Two hours."

She groaned.

"My sentiments exactly." Balancing her with one arm and the support of his knee, he yanked the covers back on the king-size bed and eased her down on the mattress. "Stay put. I'll call the doc and get some advice."

"I don't think I could go anywhere if I tried," she mumbled, a hint of amusement and false bravery in her voice.

But he was already hurrying out of the room. He knew plenty about pulling breech calves that wouldn't drop on their own, and he'd sat up many a night with a mare in labor, but a human baby—and delivering it—was totally out of his experience. And if he wasn't mistaken, just such a creature was going to be born this evening.

Snatching up the phone, he stabbed out Doc Adams's number, nearly jerking the old black phone off the hall table as he paced—and prayed.

A woman answered, and for some reason that made Brice feel calmer. "Nancy? This is Brice DeWitt over at the Flying D. Is Doc in?"

"Of course, Brice. Hold on just a moment and I'll get him for you."

Not only was Nancy Doc's wife, she was the only nurse in the county. He probably should have just saved some time and asked her what to do, but he was so rattled he wasn't thinking straight.

"Brice?" Doc's voice boomed. "Happy Almost-New Year, son."

"Same goes, Doc. Listen, I've got this lady here and her water broke—"

"Shouldn't you be calling Simmons?"

"No. The lady's a lady—I mean a woman. I don't need a vet, I need a doctor. She's having a baby."

"I see. Well, just calm down and give me the details."

How was he supposed to be calm when a tiny woman with soul-deep blue eyes was having a baby in his bedroom? "Like I know the details," he snapped, then reined in his agitation. "All I know is she's in pain and her water broke."

Doc wasn't even fazed by Brice's lapse into rudeness. "How far apart are the contractions."

"I don't—" He looked at the clock. She hadn't been here more than ten minutes, maybe less. Man alive, it felt like a lifetime. "Not far. Pretty much on top of one another."

"Hmm. Not a good sign."

"That's not what I wanted to hear. What's the chances of me getting her to the hospital?"

"Hard to say without me examining her, but with the iffy weather I wouldn't advise it. I'll come on out and have a look. Could take me a while with this fog rolling in, but I'll get there. In the meantime, remind her to do deep breathing, to focus. Nancy swears by that method. And if worse comes to worst, you've got enough experience with the animals to handle the situation. Check for signs of the head crowning and if it comes to that, use your instincts and let Mother Nature take her course."

Any calm Brice had been feeling vanished. "Check for... Oh, man, hurry." He hung up, hesitated, then called the vet just to be on the safe side. He'd get on his knees and beg if need be. Hell, he'd pay triple the emergency rate if somebody, *anybody,* would just get out here and take this problem off his hands.

He was *not* delivering a baby!

And he wasn't gonna look for... Sweat beaded his upper lip. He couldn't even bring himself to finish the thought.

By the time he got back to his bedroom, Madison Carlyle was sitting on the side of the bed, clutching the pine bedpost, tears leaking from the corners of her eyes.

His insides turned to mush. Tears unmanned him, made him feel like a big, lumbering fool.

He squatted in front of her, brushed the hair back from her face. Her eyes were unfocused and glazed with pain.

"Another one?" he asked, softly this time.

She nodded. "It's getting worse."

"Doc will be here soon." And the vet, but he didn't think she'd appreciate hearing that bit of information. "Lie back."

"I can't!" Madison clutched at her stomach and doubled over. The books on childbirth hadn't prepared her for this horrible pain. It was huge, all encompassing, clawing at her like a savage beast, wiping all thought from her head. Panting, praying, trying not to humiliate herself by screaming, she became aware a moment later of the gentle hand cupping her chin. Lifting her head, she met concerned, deep navy eyes bare inches from her own.

Maddie pulled back, embarrassed that he was witnessing her indignity.

"Easy, sunshine," he soothed. "Breathe with me now. Slow and easy." She did. "That's a girl."

Sunshine? His words were soft, his voice hypnotic. She wondered if confusion went hand in hand with labor, because she hadn't realized a man could speak with such tenderness. Especially a man as big as Brice DeWitt—and one who wasn't averse to shouting when he was off balance.

Well, he certainly seemed centered now, or maybe that's because she felt so *un*centered. With his fingers tunneled through her hair, his palms gentle against the sides of her face, he held her gaze, taking slow, deep breaths, then releasing them, encouraging her to do the same.

She knew the drill; she'd gone though the Lamaze classes, but somehow in the midst of the mind-numbing pain, she'd forgotten every lesson she'd learned.

But Brice's patience, his sturdy presence, was bringing it back to her. Their breaths mingled, in and out in unison.

Finally Maddie realized the contraction had stopped.

"Okay now?" he asked.

She nodded. "I'm really sorry about this."

He waved away her apology and opened her suitcase that he'd brought into the room. She might have objected to him rooting though her stuff, but right now she simply didn't have the energy. "You got in touch with the doctor."

"Yeah. He's on his way."

"Oh, thank goodness."

"Don't be too hasty with your thanks. The fog's rolling in pretty thick. It might take him a while to get here."

"But that's not a problem is it?"

He held up a flannel nightgown, frowned at it, then walked back toward the bed. "Maybe you should change or something," he said, instead of answering her question, making her nervous. "The bathroom's right through there."

Maddie felt her face flame. She'd applied for this job, desperate to get away. In the past few weeks, her life had literally fallen apart, and she was basically on the run, with only her car and its contents to her name. Now, on top of all that, her new employer, a stranger, a tall cowboy with a tough frown and gentle hands, was advising her to get undressed.

It was the sensible thing to do. She certainly wasn't about to chance a two-hour ride to a hospital. Still, she felt weird. "Um…isn't there a woman, uh, here?"

He pinned her with a look that was mildly accusing.

"Nope. Just a bunch of cowboys. That's why I hired you."

"Oh." She stood and reached for the gown, just as another pain slammed though her abdomen.

Brice automatically reached out to her, supporting her. Man, she was so small, it was a wonder she could even stand with the weight of her pregnancy. He hated to see anyone in pain, and he felt so helpless.

Where was this baby's father? And what kind of man would let the mother of his child go off on a cross-country trek at a time like this?

Well, not exactly cross-country, but still, his daddy had taught him that a man's supposed to take care of his woman. Provided you could get the woman to stay, that was.

Shutting his mind to that line of thought, he gazed at the tiny woman in front of him. He couldn't believe she'd actually walked a mile in labor—and in freezing temperatures. It said something about her character, and he imagined she'd need every bit of that stubbornness to get her though this night.

He knew she was making an attempt at bravery when she tried to wave him away, but he could still see the fear. And he could identify with it, because he felt it himself.

He also felt light-headed and wondered at the strange sensation. Why was he dizzy? The sound of his own breathing gave him his answer. He was inhaling and exhaling through Madison's contraction, and doing a much better job of it than she, he realized.

Ignoring her attempt to ride this one out on her own, he pried her fingers from the bedpost and stuck his face directly in her line of vision. "You're not concentrating, sunshine, and I'm about to hyperventilate trying to do it for you."

She gave him the barest hint of a smile and suddenly he felt ten feet tall.

"We can do this," he coached. "Doc says to find a focal point, and relax and concentrate on it."

In between pants, she rolled her eyes.

"Ah-ah, you're not following the program."

This time her gaze locked directly with his, defiance fairly screaming. The power of that look nearly turned his knees to water. He wanted to break the eye contact, but didn't dare for fear of spoiling her concentration. Evidently she was using *him* as her focal point. He didn't think he'd ever been anybody's lifeline like this, and he wasn't quite sure how he felt about it.

"Over?" he asked when he felt her muscles relax.

"For the moment."

"Think you can make it to the bathroom to change? Or do you need help?"

"I can manage, thanks."

He felt like an idiot hovering this way, but he didn't know what else to do. The door closed with a soft click, and for a moment, Brice stood in the middle of the room, wishing he was anywhere but here. It was ten degrees outside and the bedroom held a slight chill, but Brice felt a line of sweat dampen his spine. If somebody didn't get here soon—be he animal doctor or people doctor—Brice had the uneasy feeling he was going to have to deliver his first baby. He was out of his element and flat-out scared silly.

But he was a man of action and normally fairly adept at hiding his emotions.

He'd do what had to be done.

Resigning himself to the inevitable, he gathered up extra sheets, scissors, alcohol and an impressive first aid chest he kept in the kitchen. With the ranch being so remote, he and the men did a lot of their own doctoring.

But delivering a baby was a far cry from putting on a bandage!

MADISON STEPPED out of the bathroom, and if she hadn't been so darn scared, she would have wanted to die from embarrassment. Brice DeWitt stood by the bedside, his gaze glued to the bathroom door as though he'd been impatient for her to come out.

Lord, the guy had to be at least six foot five if he was an inch.

"You ever go out for basketball?" Oh, what an inane thing to ask! But, dear heaven, she was standing in a stranger's bedroom in a threadbare flannel nightgown.

"I played some in school."

"And the pros didn't snap you up?"

There was the barest curve to his sexy lips. "Wasn't interested. I'm a cattleman, not a jock."

Cattleman as in cowboy, she thought. Tall and in excellent physical condition. She noticed the breadth of his chest, the silver buckle at his waist, the scuffed, well-worn boots. It surprised her that the hem of his jeans bunched that way on his boots, nearly dragging the ground. For a man his size, she would have thought he'd have trouble finding a hem long enough.

Another rending pain put an end to any thoughts of sexy cowboys. In an instant, he was by her side, scooping her in his arms, settling her in the bed.

"They're getting closer, aren't they?"

"Yes. I'm scared."

He smoothed the hair back from her damp forehead. "That makes two of us." His gaze wouldn't quite meet hers when he said softly, "I've, uh, got to look."

Madison stiffened. There were several heartbeats of dead silence. She understood what he meant, but she couldn't bring herself to agree. Logic warred with emotion. Then another fierce contraction made up her mind, squeezing the breath out of her.

Fighting the pain, heart beating double time, face flaming, she nodded, slid down in the bed and raised her knees. Feeling utterly self-conscious and terrified beyond words, she stared at the blue and yellow tulips on the wallpaper, unable to look at him as he slowly lifted the hem of her gown—and encountered her cotton panties.

His frustrated groan brought her head whipping around. Well, darn it, parading around in her nightclothes was bad enough. She'd stupidly kept the underwear on to at least preserve a shred of modesty.

Now she realized what a big mistake that had been. Thankfully Brice turned his head as she slipped them off.

Gently he squeezed her knee in reassurance, then draped a blanket over her bent legs.

Tears of pain and embarrassment and gratitude over his thoughtfulness leaked from the corners of her eyes. She felt his tentative touch on her thigh and moaned.

His hand jerked. "Am I hurting you?"

"Everything's hurting me." She tried to think of anything except what he was doing…what he was *seeing*. "Do you know what you're doing?"

"Probably just enough to be dangerous. No, don't stiffen up on me. Relax."

"Easy for you to say."

He heard the fear in her voice and prayed his own wouldn't show through. "If you want to cast aspersions on the character of all men, feel free. I won't be insulted."

Maddie thought of doing just that, but another pain slammed into her like a sucker punch. Intuition told her this one meant business. Brice's muttered curse lent strength to the intuition.

"Ready or not, here we go. I think you should push with this one, Madison."

She tried, she really did. It felt as though her insides and everything along with them were ripping.

She screamed.

Brice gritted his teeth so hard his jaw ached. Either she'd been in labor longer than she'd suspected, or she was one of the lucky ones who went from start to finish in record time.

In either case, this baby was in a big hurry.

"Come on, sunshine. We're almost there." He spoke in a quiet, calm voice when all the while he wanted to scream right along with her. God Almighty, he was scared spitless. "You're doing just fine, darlin'."

"No!" She panted and gripped at the sheets until they ripped. "Briccccce!" His name tore from her on a rasping cry as the contraction peaked.

Brice watched in horror and fascination as her swollen belly shifted. He wanted to soothe her, give her focus, but his eyes remained riveted on the crowning of the baby's head. He swore to God right then and there that if the possibility existed, he'd never make a woman pregnant. No woman should have to go through this!

"Where the hell is the doctor?" he muttered.

"What's wrong?" She panted. "Is there something wrong with the baby?"

He heard the hysterical note in her voice and cursed his loose tongue. "Everything's fine. Calm down, love," he said softly.

"If you say that one more time, I'm going to hit you!"

He would have smiled if he hadn't been so preoccupied. "When this is over, I'll stand still and let you take your best shot. In the meantime…"

The grandfather clock began to chime. The noise from Dick Clark's annual New Year's Eve countdown escalated as the apple undoubtedly began its descent in Time's Square.

The baby's head was fully crowned now.

Brice began to sweat in earnest.

Voices on the television screamed, *"Ten…nine…"*

"Oh, man. Push, darlin'. Once more, I see the head. Oh, help!"

"You're doing just fine, son."

He nearly jumped out of his skin. Doc stood in the doorway, as did Jared Simmons, the vet. Brice wanted nothing more than to turn over the whole operation into Doc's capable hands, but at the moment his own hands were cradling the head of a tiny child, facedown.

"Turn it gently," Doc coached, both he and Simmons right by Brice's shoulder. "Pretend it's a calf."

Madison's groan mingled with the television revelers—as did Simmons's. Calves generally dropped on their own.

"Six…five…"

And this was definitely no calf! He turned the baby gently as instructed, his heart pounding, and felt a tiny shoulder.

"Three…two…"

Cheers erupted from the TV.

The grandfather clock drew out its twelfth chime.

A second shoulder now, tiny, slick, incredibly soft.

And before his astonished, stinging eyes, the baby slid right into his waiting hands.

Brice stared in awe as the little girl let out a lusty wail.

Looking up at Madison Carlyle, he felt a smile bathe him from the inside out, felt as though, somehow, his life would never be the same again. Powerful, possessive feelings surged through him, filling him, making him want to laugh and cry at the same time.

"Happy New Year," he said softly, emotion roughening his voice. "You've got a fine baby girl."

He tried to hand the squalling baby to Doc Adams, but the older man shook his head.

"Put her on her momma's tummy."

When Brice stood to obey the directive, Doc took his place at the end of the bed.

"Glad I was here to witness the first baby of the new year," Doc commented as Jared Simmons clapped Brice on the back. "Too bad you couldn't make it to the hospital, missy. Would have been famous—picture in the paper and all."

Madison was trembling all over from the exertion of giving birth, but the doctor's words made her shake even worse.

The *last* thing she needed was publicity focused on her and her baby.

Especially *this* baby.

Chapter Two

Brice saw a hint of sadness mixed with obvious love come over Madison's face as she stared at her baby. Something wasn't quite right here, and he wondered about it.

Her hair hung in limp, wet strands around a face pale with exhaustion. As he watched her tenderly stroke her tiny daughter's downy head, his vision blurred. Was sweat dripping in his eyes? It had to be, because he sure wasn't the emotional type.

He started to turn away, then stopped when he felt a light touch on his hand. Madison's eyes were shadowed with both pain and elation.

"Thank you," she whispered, then looked back down at her child, clearly awed, her fingers trembling as she stroked the baby's wet cheek.

"You okay?"

She nodded.

"All right you two," Doc Adams said. "You can be patting each other on the back later. Right now we got ourselves just a bit more work to do. What's your name, sweet pea?"

"Madison," Brice answered for her.

"Maddie, if you like," Madison said.

"Okay, Maddie, you're gonna feel a needle prick now. Just a little something to numb the pain. Hold on to that cowboy's hand if you're of a mind to. This is probably gonna smart some."

Brice looked down at his hands. They were a mess. He glanced around helplessly and spotted Nancy Adams hovering by her husband's shoulder. He hadn't seen her behind Doc and Jared. Of course he'd been a little preoccupied.

"Uh…Nancy, maybe you could…"

The older woman smiled and winked at him. "I never thought I'd see the day that Brice DeWitt was speechless. You go ahead and wash up. I'll get over here and act like I'm doing my job, shall I? There now, dear," she said, turning her attention to Madison. "We'll have you fixed up in no time at all, then we'll get this little daughter of yours bathed and presentable, how does that sound?"

"Good. I wouldn't turn down a healthy dose of morphine if you offered it."

Nancy laughed and expertly wrapped the baby in a blanket, then gripped Madison's hand.

Brice felt the need for flight. His bedroom had turned into a social gathering with the doctor, nurse and vet all congratulating one another, appearing to forget about him.

And in his bed was a strange woman.

No, not a stranger anymore.

After what they'd just been through together, he felt as though he'd known her for years, felt as though a bond had been forged.

Ridiculous. He barely knew her name—or anything else about her except that she wore prissy, inadequate coats and was from the city.

He nearly groaned. He wanted to be alone, wanted his life back to the way it was before Madison Carlyle and her baby daughter had interrupted it and turned everything upside down.

And he didn't particularly care for the way Jared Simmons was hovering and making jokes. Jared was a good-looking son of a gun, the most eligible bachelor in these parts—aside from Brice.

And Brice didn't consider himself eligible at all.

A sour marriage had cured him from ever wanting back in that trap.

As if in a daze, Brice made his way to the kitchen, squirted liquid soap into his callused palms and began the process of washing up. The slippery feeling of the soap reminded him of that tiny being he'd just held in his hands.

Good God, he'd couldn't believe he'd delivered a baby!

It was a miracle, plain and simple, and it had shaken him down to his toes.

Drying his hands on a dish towel, Brice stepped aside and made room for Nancy, who came bustling in, cooing nonsense to the crying infant in her arms.

"What's wrong with her?" Concern had him peering over the nurse's shoulder. In his opinion that little baby was too darned tiny to suffer any upsets that would produce such wails of agony.

"Not a thing in the world," Nancy said happily. "Except this little girl is madder than all get-out. She'll be even more so when I douse her with water."

Even as she said the words, the nurse put action to them, sticking that impossibly small head beneath the running faucet, lathering soap around the baby's hair and scrubbing it with a soft brush.

Brice felt the need to object. For God's sake, she was tossing that infant around like it was a football or something. And wasn't there a tender spot on the head someplace? An area you were supposed to be real careful about?

"Aren't you hurting her?" The baby was pitiful looking, all red and wrinkled, eyes squeezed tightly shut, chin quivering, emitting sounds that resembled a sick kitten. Then again that queer melting sensation in the region of his heart kicked in, and he decided she was pretty cute for such a miniature thing.

Nancy chuckled. "No. Babies are a lot tougher than they look."

Brice knew he was crowding the nurse, but he couldn't seem to help himself. He felt possessive, territorial, wanting to touch, yet afraid.

He dogged Nancy's steps, supervising every aspect of this

hurried bath, then made severe objecting noises when Nancy blithely jabbed an injection needle into a tiny thigh.

"Oh, man…" For a moment, Brice thought he, too, might cry—or faint—as he watched the delayed reaction of the baby, noticed the instant pain registered in its brain, bringing forth a chin-quivering wail that weakened his knees. He glared at the woman who'd had the audacity to perform such a cruel act.

"To clot the blood," Nancy explained, laughing at Brice's fierce expression. "Vitamin K."

Brice watched in astonished awe as the nurse poked and prodded, bending the baby's wrist almost double, running her fingers over the outer shell of its tiny ears. Twice he reached out to stop what appeared to be torture, then stuffed his hands in his pockets. Nancy didn't have a mean bone in her body.

"By feeling the cartilage in an infant's ears, we can tell whether or not certain internal organs are developed."

Brice was impressed despite himself, then immediately went on guard when the woman bundled the baby tightly in a blanket and held her out, expecting him to take over.

He jerked his hands out of his pockets as though she'd just hollered, "Think fast." "I don't…"

"Might as well go on and take her, son." Doc Adams ambled into the kitchen and began washing up at the sink. "You did most of the work, now comes the part that's pure-dee joy."

He'd held her before, when she'd been wet and slippery. But that had been instinct and necessity. He hadn't even thought about it. Now, with her all cleaned up and wrapped like a mummy, he was scared to death to touch her. What if he dropped her or hurt her? His hands were almost bigger than her whole body.

Doc Adams chuckled. "You won't drop her, boy."

Awkward at first, then with increasing confidence, Brice accepted the warm life he'd had a hand in bringing into the world. She fidgeted a bit but didn't cry. Carefully he reached down to move the blanket out of her face.

His heart slammed against his ribs, and he was filled with a sense of almost unbearable incredulity, for at that moment, the tiny child wrapped her fingers around one of his, effectively and forever wrapping herself around his heart.

Well, princess, you're about the best, most unspoiled accomplishment I've ever had.

"You did a fine job with her," Doc said. "First baby of the new year. Born right here on the Flying D. Frank would have been tickled."

Yeah, Brice thought. Frank DeWitt had enjoyed kids, had been a good father.

He just hadn't been good at getting women to stay.

Like father like son.

Brice didn't want to get attached to this baby. Just like he didn't want to get attached to her mother. A little devil inside him taunted that it was too late.

"Madison?" he asked. "How is she?"

"Tired, but she's a trooper. Who is she, by the way?"

"The new housekeeper."

Doc's brows rose. "Be a couple of weeks before she feels up to working."

"More than that," Nancy put in. "She told me to let someone know that there are baby supplies in her car. You'll need to go after them pretty soon. I brought a couple of infant diapers over, but that won't last you long."

Brice nodded. "I'll see to it." He wondered what would cause a woman in advanced pregnancy to apply for a live-in job, to show up in the middle of the night in a fussy, inadequate coat and a car full of baby supplies.

"Better see to getting this baby in her mama's arms," Jared Simmons said. "The lady's getting anxious."

Brice looked around the room, hoping someone would offer to take over. Standing still with the baby in his arms was one thing. He'd have felt more secure sitting down. But walking and holding at the same time?

"Go on, boy," Doc urged. "I'll come back in a few days and check on them."

That brought his head up. "A few days? Shouldn't we move them to the hospital or something?" She'd said there was no *Mr.* Carlyle, but that only meant she wasn't married. Obviously this baby had a father. A father who could well show up to claim them.

"No need. Both mother and baby are healthy. And I'm only a phone call away." Doc gathered up his medical bag and slung an arm across his wife's shoulders. "Besides, Nancy and I could use a little privacy. We missed our New Year's kiss."

Nancy tittered and elbowed her husband, but profound love shone clearly in her hazel eyes as she gave her husband a peck on the cheek. "That'll hold you for a while." Then she moved to Brice and placed a kiss on his jaw. "Happy New Year, Brice. And congratulations on the new addition to the Flying D."

Before he could set her straight, tell her that this baby would *not* be staying at the Flying D, the back door opened.

"What in tarnation's going on? Looks like a dang cattlemen's convention in the yard out there with all the pickups." The old cowboy whipped off his battered hat, causing tufts of gray hair to stick out above his ears. "A few puppies being born on New Year's Eve don't require the vet and the Doc and—what the Sam Hill are you holding, boy?" Moe Bertelli's bushy brows slammed together.

"Puppies?" Brice asked, completely bypassing Moe's question. He hadn't realized the collie was due. No wonder Jax had whined until Brice had let him out to go to the bunkhouse. At the time he'd felt abandoned by his dog, which had only added to his loneliness over facing the new year. He'd taken it personally that his faithful Lab hadn't wanted to stick around.

"That ain't no puppy."

Brice's brain was a little slow keeping up. "No, I didn't mean the baby, I meant—"

"Sally birthed three pups," Moe interrupted. "Jax is a proud papa. But who the devil delivered this?" His words were gruff, but his gnarled hands were gentle as he pulled back the blanket and took a peek.

"The housekeeper," Jared Simmons supplied.

Moe spared the vet a pitying glare. "Lavinia's too danged old to have babies. Besides, she already left. I know that for a fact cuz my stomach's not as cast iron as it used to be." He looked back at Brice, clearly annoyed that he was out of the information loop. Moe liked to know everything that was going on.

"The *new* housekeeper showed up." Puppies born at midnight, too? Man alive, everywhere he turned, babies were sprouting.

"Humph. Looks like more 'an that showed up. Scrawny little thing."

Brice felt insulted on the baby's behalf. He half turned, scowling. "She's hardly an hour old."

"A she? Well that'll be just fine. We'll put her on a pony before she crawls. Teach her what's what right off."

"No," Brice said. "It won't be just fine. She's not staying." He pictured it in his mind, though—a little girl with wheat blond hair like her mother's, pigtails flopping as she sat atop a trotting pony.

"Thought you said her ma was the new housekeeper."

Brice looked at the man who'd been like a second father to him for as long as he could remember. Had the arthritis affected the old geezer's brain? "This is no place for a woman and a kid."

"Why the hell not?" Moe sent the scowl right back.

Brice didn't like the way everyone in the room was looking at him. As though they could see into his chest, were picturing his heart broken. As though they were remembering the days after his mother had left, then again the days after Sharon had left.

Well, fine. If they were remembering, then they had to realize that Madison Carlyle couldn't stay.

Wouldn't stay.

At least not for long.

And that being the case, he had no business feeling attached.

To this baby, or to her mother—who was probably at this minute wondering what they'd done with her newborn.

The baby mewled and gave a tiny cry that sounded like a cough that wouldn't quite form.

Brice's nerves stood on end. "I better get her to Madison. Thanks for coming Doc—Jared," he added at the last minute. The handsome young vet looked as though he wouldn't mind staying for a while. For some reason Brice wasn't thrilled with the longing glances the man kept sending in the way of the bedroom.

Feeling utterly stupid, he took a careful step, then another. So far so good. Walking and holding at the same time wasn't as hard as he'd thought.

MADDIE FELT as though she'd been run through an old-fashioned laundry wringer. The adrenaline generated by the frantic road trip from Dallas to Wyoming had ebbed.

And here she was, on a remote cattle ranch where no one would think to look for her.

And she had a daughter.

More exhausted than she could ever remember being, her arms still ached to hold her child.

She looked up as Brice DeWitt paused in the doorway, his head barely clearing the jamb. He seemed even bigger standing there holding her tiny daughter, looking awkward and awed all at the same time.

She smiled and held out her arms.

He moved forward carefully, leaned down and placed the baby in her arms. He smelled of soap and of baby.

Immediately she began to unwrap the blanket from her child, needing to look, to memorize, unable to believe the swell of love that rose in her, consumed her.

This tiny miracle had come from her body.

And she was absolutely perfect.

"Everything appears to be there," Brice said softly. "Nancy gave her a pretty good going over."

"Why is there a Band-Aid on her thigh?"

"Got her first shot. Nancy had that syringe popped in before I could stop her. And believe me, sunshine, I'd have tried."

Maddie smiled at his look of horror, yet felt ridiculously weepy. Her eyes had been leaking so much in the past few hours, it was a wonder her contact lenses were still in place.

"Thank you, Brice. For my daughter"

He shrugged. "All in a day's work."

"I doubt that. And I'm sorry I yelled at you."

He reached out as though to touch the baby, then balled his fingers into a fist and pulled back. "No problem. I'd have done worse, and in much stronger language. At least we know your little girl comes by her strong lungs rightfully. So…you thought about a name?"

"I've always liked Gabriella." She noticed his frown. "What? You don't like it?" For some reason, his approval over her baby's name seemed important.

"It's an okay name, I suppose."

"But?"

"But people will call her Gabby. What if she's a shy little kid and feels like people are teasing her when she talks?"

Maddie hadn't thought of that. And she knew plenty about the hurtfulness of teasing. She'd been shuffled through so many different schools and so many different foster families she'd never really had a chance to form friends, allies. She'd always been the odd little girl who wore thick glasses and had no real parents.

Homeless four eyes.

A sense of fierce protectiveness welled up in her. Her little daughter would have roots. Nobody, *nobody* would take this sweet baby from her. She would have love and every advantage Madison could provide. And that included a special name, a beautiful name.

"What about Abigail?"

"Abigail," he repeated softly. "Pretty. Too bad Doc's already gone. He could have filled out the birth certificate and got it ready to go to the state. Doc says it's a big deal to be the first baby of the new year."

Maddie tightened her arms around her daughter. She'd forgotten about filing paperwork with the state.

Records were traceable.

And the Covingtons would be looking for birth records.

Anxiety winged through her as perspiration beaded her upper lip.

"Hey, you okay?"

"I'm fine. Just tired. I hate to be any more trouble, but is there anyone who can get Abbe's stuff out of my car? She'll need diapers, clothes, blankets."

"I'll get it. And I'll call Leonard about the car. He'll have it towed in to the garage. Might be a little tough to budge him from football games, but it shouldn't take him more that a couple of days to diagnose your car troubles. Then you can be on your way."

She felt the bottom drop out of her stomach. "But…the job."

The desperate look that came over her face made Brice feel as though he'd just stepped on a kitten. "Ranch duties are hard work, sunshine. This isn't really the job for you."

"I'm not afraid of hard work."

"Just caring for that baby is going to take most of your energy—"

"I can handle it, Brice. I need this job."

He frowned. "What are you hiding from?"

"I'm not—" She stopped, took a breath. "I have a child to support. I need to work." She gave him a defiant look. "You hired me."

"Before I knew you were pregnant."

"So? You don't look like the discriminating type to me."

He felt his temper rise, battled it down. "I'm not."

"Then give me a chance. I won't let you down."

He'd heard those words before. With regard to him, that particular promise usually got broken.

The baby scrunched up her face and worked her little self into a snit—probably because he'd agitated her mother.

Brice ran a hand around the back of his neck. He couldn't throw them out. Madison Carlyle was hiding something, but at the moment she didn't appear willing to impart what that was.

And Doc said she should rest for a couple of weeks. He could make it that long, couldn't he? Two weeks wasn't nearly enough time to become attached to something or someone he couldn't keep.

"We'll talk more when you're on your feet."

She astonished him by struggling to a sitting position and attempting to swing her legs over the side of the mattress.

He shot forward, hovering, not knowing whether to grab her or the baby or both. "What are you doing?"

"Getting on my feet."

"Don't be cute. I didn't mean right this minute."

"I've never been cute in my life."

That statement, along with her flat, unemotional tone, surprised him even more than her trying to get up. Clearly she was referring to looks. And clearly she didn't realize her appeal. Oh, she looked a little wrung out at the moment, what woman wouldn't after childbirth. But even though her sunny hair had gone limp and her complexion was pale, even though she wore an old flannel nightgown with tiny pink rosebuds on it, she made him want to just stop and stare.

And she made him long to ask her to stay.

"What do you do?"

"Do?"

"For a living—when you're not applying for housekeeping positions, that is."

"I'm an accountant."

An idea formed in his head, and as much as he told himself to stay away, to send her away, to not get involved in her secrets and her soul-deep blue eyes, he heard himself saying, "Then we'll start there."

"Excuse me?"

"Housekeeping duties and lugging huge pots and pans are out of the question right now. I'm behind on the ranch books. Maybe you can make some sense out of them."

Her eyes brightened, making him feel as though he'd just given an orphan a much-coveted Christmas present.

"Thank you."

"Don't jump the gun. It's only temporary." He scowled at her. Deliberately. And the fool woman gave him a bright smile for his efforts.

He had to get out of this room before he offered her the moon. "I'll get the baby stuff out of your car." His tone was abrupt, and so was his exit.

He pulled the bedroom door partially closed behind him and leaned against the wall, wondering what had possessed him to offer her a bookkeeping job.

He was just about to move away from the slightly opened door when he heard her soft voice.

"Oh, Abbe, Mama's here. I promise everything will be fine. *We'll* be fine. Wyoming is a nice place to live. It was too dark to see much, but I'm sure it'll be great. I promise you, baby, you'll have roots. Even if it's not here, you and I will make our way in life. And you'll always know you're loved. I never knew love when I was growing up, but you will.

"And birthdays and Christmas and all the other holidays will be grand. You wait and see. I used to pretend that holidays weren't any big deal. I learned not to expect much, so I couldn't be let down. But I wasn't really strong that way, Abbe. I *did* hope. And I yearned. And I was hurt when nobody remembered me.

"Don't you worry, though. That's never going to happen to you. You'll never experience a sadness like that," she said fiercely. "It's you and me, baby. We'll have a happy life, even if you never have much in the way of material things. We'll be strong together."

Brice strained to hear as her voice softened to a whisper.

"Nobody will take you away from me. It's just a hunch, but I think Brice DeWitt is like a gift to us. A birthday gift, on your birth day."

Oh, man. He rubbed his chest as though his heart hurt. After listening to that heartrending vow, how could he ask her to leave?

And who was threatening to take her baby away?

Chapter Three

Brice pushed away from the wall, retrieved Madison's purse from the front room and went out through the kitchen, jamming his hat on his head. Jax met him at the back door and gave a soft bark.

"Now you decide to show up," he said to the golden Labrador. "Congratulations, old man. I hear you're a father." Jax wagged his tail and nudged Brice's thigh as though apologizing for abandoning him. "Okay, you're forgiven. You had a good reason for ringing in the new year someplace else."

"Where you headin' off to in the middle of the night?" Moe asked, causing Brice to nearly jump out of his skin. He hadn't realized the old cowboy was sitting at the kitchen table.

"Shouldn't you be turning in, Bertelli?"

"Durn straight I should be. With all the commotion, I'm a bit high strung. Then you come in here yammerin' to the dog like he knows what you're sayin'."

"He does."

"Humph. Where you going?"

"To get Madison's things out of her car." He hadn't felt the need to account for his comings and goings in a long time. The events of the night must have made him mellow.

"Didn't see no car in the drive."

"It broke down out on the highway."

"So how'd she get here?"

"Walked."

"Walked?" Moe nearly upset his coffee cup when he slapped a palm against the table. "While havin' a baby?"

"The baby waited until she got in the front hall. There's a mess, by the way. Careful if you walk that way."

"I'll see to it."

"No. You go on to bed. I'll be up for a while yet."

Moe gave him a stubborn look. Brice knew that look. The man would get the mop the minute Brice was out of sight. He started to go take care of the matter himself, but he figured he had better see what kind of baby supplies were in Madison's car first. Besides, Moe got real ornery when Brice made any attempt to go easy on him. Moe Bertelli had more pride than was good for him.

"Get," Moe ordered. "I'll keep an ear peeled for the mama and little one while you're gone."

Knowing he wouldn't be able to budge the old cowboy once his mind was made up, Brice nodded and snapped his fingers for Jax, who happily followed him outside and scrambled into the cab of the truck.

The cold air stung his neck, and he hunched his shoulders beneath his sheepskin-lined jacket, waiting for the Chevy's heater to kick in.

The headlights barely made a dent in the dense fog. The smell of animals and manure permeated the air, made stronger by the veil of thick fog. He negotiated the long drive by rote, intimately familiar with each pothole and rut, relying on the odometer to let him know when he was nearing the highway.

Madison had said the car was about a mile away. Did that include the quarter-mile driveway?

No, it didn't.

The odometer read a tenth short of two miles when he spotted the dark-colored Nissan sitting like a sad waif just off the road, its right side hugging the split-rail fence as though seeking warmth.

Once again he thought of Madison's strength and determination.

And her passionate words to her baby daughter.

Opening the purse in search of car keys—he figured a city girl would probably have locked the car—his hand paused as it landed on her wallet.

He battled with himself for several minutes. Normally he didn't like to pry. Let folks be what they would be.

But curiosity got the better of him. Besides, the woman was in his bed. He ought to at least know her vital statistics.

Flipping open the leather clutch, he scanned the driver's license. Five foot three, blue eyes, blond hair, wears glasses, born February 4, 1970. That would make her twenty-nine next month.

He remembered her sad account of learning not to expect much for birthdays. Hell, what would that be like? Brice had grown up without a mother, but he'd had his father and Moe to dote on him. He'd had roots, the land. And not once had anyone forgotten his or his brother, Kyle's, birthday.

He'd have to make sure no one forgot Madison Carlyle's this year.

"Stay here, boy," he said to Jax, then got out to unload Madison's car. She'd said she had all she'd need for herself and the baby.

It made his insides clench to think a person's life could fit into the back seat and trunk of a compact. And what was there was pitifully sparse in his opinion. Maybe the rest of her belongings were in storage?

The absolute essentials were there, including an infant carrier that doubled as a car seat. But what about a baby bed? he wondered, feeling idiotic as he scanned the cramped interior for any large items he might have overlooked.

Every newborn baby needed a crib, didn't she? And flying things—a mobile, that's what they were—twirling happily. And toys.

He shook his head and retrieved a fuzzy white stuffed lamb, a kit with pacifiers and thermometers and a couple of bottles....

Only a couple. That meant…ah man, he'd forgotten that new mothers nursed babies.

He put that thought out of his head as he transferred suit-cases and bags into the bed of the truck. It only took him three trips.

This wasn't acceptable.

As soon as he got back to the ranch, he'd get out the JCPen-ney catalogue. Via overnight UPS, they could have a nursery set up by the third day of the new year.

Even if it was only for a little while, baby Abbe deserved a decent bed to sleep in.

AFTER DOING LITTLE MORE than lying around the past two days since Abbe's birth, Madison was determined to get up and explore the house, to attempt a few duties in order to pay Brice back for his help and hospitality.

Because she wasn't here to accept hospitality.

She was here to work. Surely she could manage a little cook-ing, maybe even take a look at the ranch accounts.

Abbe made snuffling noises, and Maddie moved to the dresser drawer Brice had rigged up as a temporary bassinet. She'd thought she would get settled, work hard and make her-self indispensable before she broached the subject of needing to purchase nursery furniture.

Well, baby Abbe had messed up her timetable a bit. She smiled as she lifted the sweet baby into her arms and nuzzled an incredibly soft cheek. Abbe's mouth opened like a baby bird's, seeking nourishment.

"Okay, okay. Let's get you changed." Her hands shook as she wrestled with the cloth diaper and pins. "I'll get faster at this, Abbe. Just bear with me."

Finished with the task, perspiring from both nerves and the effort, she sat on the edge of the mattress, opened her robe, then winced as Abbe latched on to her nipple.

It felt like a thousand white-hot needles were piercing her

breasts. Surely this part would get easier with time. As Abbe sucked, tears stung Maddie's eyes.

Lord, she was exhausted, and she hadn't done a blessed thing for two days. Cute as she was, Abbe didn't sleep more than twenty minutes at a stretch. And Madison felt guilty that nursing wasn't the joy she'd expected it to be.

But that wasn't the baby's fault.

There were a lot of things that weren't as she'd expected.

Brice DeWitt, for one.

He was so strikingly...*male.* Surely it was the flood of extra childbirth hormones that caused her to catch her breath every time he walked into the room.

She'd appropriated his bedroom, and she felt bad about that. She knew he left in the mornings by five and spent long hours on the land. Then he checked on her, and even showed up several times during the night when Abbe cried. Neither one of them were getting any sleep.

Once she had the baby changed, *again,* and resting back in the makeshift bed, she showered and pulled on a pair of sweats. She hadn't gained that much weight with the pregnancy and had expected to be back in her clothes fairly soon.

Another underestimation on her part—in a long and growing list.

How in the world had her life taken such a devastating turn? She'd had it all planned out. That's what she did—planned, made lists, left little or nothing to fate. That way there was less chance of being let down, less chance of surprises blindsiding her.

Well, she'd been blindsided—big-time. Everything had changed. She'd given up her rented house with its picket fences and happy flowers—the dream cottage she'd intended to buy. She'd chosen it because it was in a good neighborhood, with good schools and a great little yard for her child to play in—a child that had been planned for, whom she'd fallen in love with the moment the test had come back positive, the joyous moment when she'd realized that the anonymous sperm had indeed mated with her egg.

Feeling as though she were living her own carefully written fairy tale, she'd turned the third bedroom of her house into an office and had run her CPA business out of it. She'd worked hard to build up clientele and a savings account, had felt so smug at her success—that she'd be able to be a stay-at-home mom and provide a good living.

But all that had turned to dust overnight. The Covingtons had seen to it.

She wasn't even sure if they had legal rights, but she'd been too scared to wait around and find out. She'd packed up and left before court papers could be served.

She couldn't take the chance that the Covingtons were bluffing.

But now she had to make a living. Her savings account was fairly healthy, but it would only last so long. She didn't want to have to go out and find a job that would require leaving her baby with a sitter—that's why she'd designed a home business in the first place.

And Brice's ad, like a gift from heaven, had seemed like the perfect solution. So she'd left the computers behind, put the furniture in storage, given up her dream house...and prayed that Wyoming would be the safe haven she and her child needed.

But it was obvious that Brice DeWitt wasn't keen on her staying for long, didn't think she had what it took to survive on his ranch.

Well, she'd just have to prove him wrong. She might be little, but she was tenacious; she had more determination than most people.

She'd learned that the hard way.

Picking up the baby, drawer and all, she made her way to the kitchen. The coffee in the pot was cold, and a quick search of her surroundings didn't produce a microwave.

Goodness, how did anyone survive without the essential appliances?

She rummaged through cabinets, trying to familiarize herself with the room she was supposed to spend time in now. What in the world had she been thinking? That there'd be frozen hungry-man dinners in the freezer, and pantries stocked with boxes of breakfast cereal? Evidently the people on this ranch didn't believe in quick-and-easy conveniences. And though it had been dark when she'd driven in the other night, she knew for certain that there wasn't a McDonald's or Taco Bell within fifty miles.

She popped a piece of bread in the toaster and brewed a fresh pot of coffee, absently drumming her fingers against the porcelain sink as she gazed out the window.

The sky was the color of stone, blanketed by billowing clouds that promised snow. Frigid air blew through the slightly open window, making her shiver. She reached up to close it, her hand stilling when she saw a lone rider galloping across the barren field toward one of the outbuildings.

Brice.

She knew it was him from his height in the saddle alone. Her stomach gave a funny tickle. She'd seen cowboys before, but mostly the spiffed-up kind at the local honky-tonks in Dallas.

This man was a working cowboy. He sat atop a gorgeous roan, moving with the animal in perfect harmony, as though he'd spent most of his life in the saddle. Which he probably had.

Dismounting, he passed the horse's reins to another man who came out of the barn, then gazed off toward the main highway.

Madison looked in that direction, too, astonished to see a brown delivery truck spewing gravel beneath its tires as it barreled down the lane.

UPS delivers to the middle of nowhere? The sight was so incongruous, so unexpected, that silent alarms went off in her brain, an intuitive warning that had dogged her every waking moment for the past few weeks.

Her heart lurched and she ducked away from the window,

automatically reaching for the baby. Surely they hadn't found her. She'd been so careful.

Gently, trying not to wake her, she held Abbe close, feeling like a protective mama bear whose cub was threatened.

Leaving the dresser drawer bassinet sitting on the oak kitchen table, she stood in indecision for several minutes, then stole into the living room, heading for the bedroom.

Halfway through the room, she had second thoughts. She shouldn't have left the makeshift baby bed behind. Darn it, she wasn't used to second-guessing her every move. Indecision clawed at her.

Then the front door swung open with a crash and it took every ounce of strength she possessed not to squeak in alarm. Cold air rushed in, and Maddie felt frozen to the spot, like a deer caught in headlights.

The first thing she saw was Brice DeWitt's butt.

He'd discarded his coat somewhere between the barn and the house. A pair of leather chaps were tied just under the curve of his rear, very nicely displaying that particular part of his anatomy. He backed into the room, holding one end of a large box. The other end was supported by a deliveryman in a recognizable brown uniform.

Her initial nerves over unexpected company ebbed a bit.

The delivery guy grinned, set down his end of the carton and gave an exuberant wave. "Hi, there! Looks like Christmas comes late out here. Lucky you, I've got five more boxes."

Brice whipped around, not expecting Madison to be up, feeling embarrassed by his impulsive purchases. He'd definitely gone overboard with the catalogue.

"What are you doing out of bed?"

She was wearing her round spectacles today. A slim blond brow arched above the wire frame. "You're out working. I figured it was time for me to get with the program, too."

He started toward her, then stopped. He smelled like a horse. And she looked entirely too fragile to touch, as though she'd suffered a fright but was valiantly trying to hide it.

"Is everything okay? The baby?"

"We're fine." She waved a hand toward the huge carton, and the others that were now stacked beside it. "What's all this?"

He turned and signed the delivery ticket.

"Enjoy!" the UPS guy said, then jogged back to his truck.

Brice shut the door and pulled out the order form. Had he actually ordered *all* this stuff? Hell, the baby wasn't even his kid. For all he knew some guy would show up at the front door and claim Madison and Abbe.

According to the invoice the order had been split. Good God. Madison was going to think he was crazy. This wasn't even the entire shipment.

"Come see for yourself," he finally answered, shucking his heavy gloves and ripping open the biggest box.

Madison took a tentative step forward, then another, and stared over his shoulder, speechless.

Plastic foam peanuts littered the floor as Brice tugged parts of a maple Jenny Lind crib from the box. Next came a mattress with lambs and bears frolicking across the vinyl surface.

A lump formed in her throat as she touched the smooth wood. Dear Lord, she was going to cry. What was *with* these leaky eyes of hers?

"Well? What do you think? I'll have to put it together. But if you don't like it, we can exchange it for something different."

She had trouble finding her voice, getting words past the emotion in her throat. "I love it," she said softly. "It's exactly what I would have picked. But…why?"

"Why what?" He looked uncomfortable as he opened another box.

"Why did you do this?"

He shrugged. "The kid needed a decent bed. It's not right that she's sleeping in a drawer." He extracted a set of bumper pads that sported the same lamb and teddy bear motif as the mattress.

"Brice…I don't know what to say. You shouldn't have."

He cut through the packing tape of the remaining boxes without looking at their contents, then stood, towering over her.

"There's five bedrooms in this house, two of them sitting empty. Might as well turn one into a nursery for a while."

For a while. Well, at least it was a step in the right direction. A least he hadn't started in on her about leaving again, about her not being right for the job. The fact that he'd purchased baby furniture was a good thing, it bought her time. Time to prove that she could handle the ranch chores.

Even if he didn't own a microwave.

Now, more than ever, she was determined to pull her weight, to pay him back. She reached out and placed a hand on his rock-hard forearm. "Thank you."

He shrugged again, his gaze lingering on where her hand rested against his arm. This man surprised her. He'd delivered her baby, slipped into her bedroom in the middle of the night when Abbe cried, bought her furniture. Yet he kept his emotions hidden behind a mask, making her ache to know what he was really thinking, feeling.

One minute he was telling her she wasn't right for the job, and the next he was buying out of mail-order catalogues as though expecting forever.

"How did you manage all this?" she asked.

His navy gaze met hers. "I think I'm on every catalogue mailing list in the country. Comes in handy when I need more than what the feed store in town carries."

"Well, thank you for thinking of it. I'll pay you back, of course. Just let me know the invoice amount." She mentally pictured the balances in her accounts, and hoped he was a bargain shopper.

He scowled and tugged at the brim of his black hat, a gesture that seemed more habitual than conscious. "I'm going to pretend you didn't say that."

"Why? I can't let you be buying things for us."

He took a step closer, deliberately, it seemed, to point out that he was much bigger than her. "Think you can stop me?"

She bit her bottom lip, but couldn't stop the smile that formed or the bubble of laughter that worked its way to her throat. If this tall, tough, dreamy-looking cowboy thought he could intimidate her with his sheer size, he had a lot to learn. She'd faced down scarier adversaries in her life. The fierce scowl was a nice touch, though.

The barest hint of amusement flared in his eyes when she stood her ground. "Smart," he murmured. "As well as beautiful."

She nearly rolled her eyes. She was wearing ancient sweats that bagged at the knees and the seat, and she didn't have on a speck of makeup behind the lenses of her glasses.

"Obviously you're as sleep deprived as I am." She tucked a strand of hair behind her ear, wishing she'd taken more time to fix it.

The smell of earth and animals emanated from him, making her knees weak. She glanced at the shipping cartons then back to him. "I would have never pictured you thumbing through or shopping with catalogues."

His gaze lingered on her mouth. "I'm fairly resourceful. When I see something I want, I usually get it."

For some reason, she didn't think he was talking about mail-order merchandise. Nervous for no good reason, she licked her lips. Her smile faltered when she saw the sudden heat in his dark eyes. Her arms went weak and trembly, making her fear dropping the baby. For the life of her, she couldn't move or make her voice work.

The grandfather clock chimed the hour. A ranch hand shouted outside, and horses' hooves thundered.

He took a step closer, bent his head ever so slightly.

Her eyes widened. Dear Lord, he had the look of a man with a keen thirst. Was he actually about to kiss her? Was she going to let him?

Oh, this was unfamiliar territory. At one time she'd played

the game—the man-woman game—but it had been a long time ago. She was rusty, unsure of reading the signals correctly.

Her heart pumped and her stomach fluttered. Something cold trickled against her breasts.

Abbe squirmed and fussed.

And just that quickly, the odd moment was broken.

As though she'd imagined the whole charged episode, his gaze shifted to the baby.

"Her eyes are open."

Maddie looked down. Yes, Abbe was awake—as usual. And as usual, when she looked at her baby daughter, love, powerful and all consuming, squeezed her.

On the heels of that emotion, though, came acute horror.

The front of her sweatshirt sported twin damp spots.

It seemed she was destined to be put in highly embarrassing situations with this man.

"Um…maybe I should go change…her."

His lips curved ever so slightly. "Yeah." He backed up a step, pulled his gloves out of his hip pocket and looked everywhere but at her. "I've got a fence down in the back section I need to get to. I'll put the crib together later."

She nodded, started toward the bedroom, then stopped. "Brice?"

"Yeah?"

He'd already turned and had his hand on the front door-knob—which of course gave her another excellent visual feast of his sexy butt framed by buff-colored chaps. She nearly lost her train of thought.

He cleared his throat and her gaze snapped up to his, her face flaming. For Pete's sake, she was *not* the sort of woman who had to pick her tongue up off the floor!

Obviously, breast feeding had sucked the brains right out of her head.

What had she been about to ask? Oh, yes, the boxes.

"Would you mind if I, uh, looked at what you ordered?" She

hoped her wistfulness didn't show. But darn it, gifts were a rare occurrence in her life.

"Be my guest. They're yours."

"Thank you," she said softly. Those two words were packed with more meaning than he could know.

He looked as though he was about to say something else, then changed his mind and pulled on his gloves.

"Don't lift anything heavy. I'll take care of it when I get back." He touched the brim of his hat, the gesture reminding her of romance and gallantry. She half expected him to add a shyly abrupt, *ma'am* as she'd seen countless times in Westerns, but he just pulled open the door and walked through.

Maddie stood right where she was for several minutes, the damp circles on the front of her sweatshirt growing wider.

At last she looked down at her wide-eyed baby daughter.

"Here's your first piece of motherly advice, pumpkin. When you become the first woman president, you'll have to introduce a bill to Congress making leather chaps illegal to wear in public. Especially if the cowboy in question turns his back. It's enough to make a tough woman swoon. And that of course, could cause all manner of mayhem—wrecks on the expressway, collisions at stop lights…heart attacks. Definitely dangerous."

Abbe yawned.

"You're right. Forget the law."

Chapter Four

"Good Lord, I've only been here three days and look what I've done." The kitchen was doing an excellent imitation of a disaster area, and if it were possible, Maddie felt worse than the room looked.

"Shhh, Abbe, don't cry, sweetie." She paced and jiggled and hummed—all the while looking at the mess she'd made.

Cooking from scratch was not her strong suit. The biscuits were charred, the stew meat tough as cow's hide, and the gravy the consistency of lumpy water. It was too late to do anything about the biscuits—she'd just have to improvise with bread. As for the lumps, they could be fished out if she could ever find the danged slotted spoon.

For the hundredth time in the past forty-five minutes, she longed for her coveted microwave, which was sitting in a lonely storage unit in Dallas. A quick zap and the undercooked stew meat would at least be chewable.

So much for her vow of making herself indispensable, she thought. One look at this mess and, car fixed or not, Brice would probably drive her off his property himself.

Right now, though, she had a more immediate concern, because Abbe simply wouldn't settle down.

And Maddie was on the verge of bawling right along with her unhappy daughter, who fussed and fidgeted in a sling that was draped over Maddie's shoulder.

"Please, baby. Tell Mama what you want." She opened her

blouse and held her breath, her eyes stinging as Abbe sucked. Sweat beaded her lip as painful chills pricked her skin.

The kitchen door opened and Maddie's head snapped up.

Brice came in, trailed by three cowboys, bringing with them the smell of animals and earth and crisp Wyoming air. In the process of peeling off hats, gloves and winter coats, it was a moment before Brice looked up.

When he did, he came to an abrupt halt, causing the other three cowboys to plow into his back like a choreographed skit in a slapstick comedy.

"Holy smoke! What happened in here?"

"Dinner."

"Dinner?" he repeated, looking at the charred biscuits, the flour dusting the floor and counters like new snow, the carrot peelings streaking the porcelain sink orange.

His dark blue gaze went to the sling that shielded Abbe—as well as Maddie's breasts—from view.

"What in tarnation are you yammerin' about?" Moe complained. "And stoppin' in the middle of the door like that, you 'bout rattled my teeth loose." He looked over Brice's shoulder. "Oh, evenin', Miss Maddie."

By now the other two cowboys were shuffling their feet and trying to figure out where to look—or not to look.

Moe turned on them. "Get," he ordered. "Cain't ya see the lady needs privacy?"

"No," Maddie said, embarrassed, but sure that all her body parts were covered. She wouldn't cause the men to change their routine on her account.

Of course, they might think twice once they tasted the dinner.

Brice took another look around the kitchen, which appeared pretty unrecognizable at the moment. Even he hadn't managed to do this much damage in an hour.

And Madison didn't look much better. She resembled a rain cloud about to burst, yet was putting on a brave front.

"You shouldn't be trying to cook so soon," he said, thinking that was a hell of an understatement. He lifted the lid on a pot where vegetables swam in dung-colored water. It smelled decent enough. The biscuits were another matter entirely. Definitely a lost cause. "I appreciate it, though. We're starving, right guys?"

The trio still standing in the doorway murmured their agreement.

Madison gave a muffled laugh, causing him to swing around.

Apology and amusement shone in her eyes. "I don't usually make such a mess of things. I'm normally very organized. However, before you speak too hastily about appreciation, you might consider calling the pizza man."

He appreciated a woman who could laugh at her mistakes. He'd thought she was on the verge of tears because she'd muffed the dinner—and totaled his kitchen in the bargain. But that wasn't the case. She was simply exhausted, understandably wrung out because of the baby and recent childbirth.

He felt a grin tug at his lips. "Pizza parlors don't deliver out this far."

Her blond brows rose above her round spectacles. "Pity. They don't operate on the same motto as the UPS guys, hmm?"

Brice knew the delivery truck had been here again today. He'd seen it when he'd been rescuing a dogie from a briar patch. "Was the shipment complete?"

"I certainly hope so. Did you order every item in the baby section of the JCPenney catalogue?"

He felt his ears burn and turned to grab a loaf of bread off the counter. The other men in the room were shooting him speculative looks, and he knew he'd take a lot more ribbing before all was said and done. But what the hell. It was his ranch; he was the boss. He could order any damned thing he wanted.

"I might have missed a thing or two. So what came today?"

"A fanciful mobile with plush lambs and teddy bears, and a plastic bathtub with a sponge insert shaped like a duck."

"That should be it for a while." He stepped aside as Moe opened the refrigerator and took out a tub of butter and a jar of Letty Springer's homemade jelly. Dan Shuller and Randy Toval still hovered just inside the doorway.

Moe tossed a look at the cowhands. "If you're not gonna get, then sit. Or better yet, make yerselves useful and set some eatin' trays on the table."

"I'll do it," Madison said, adjusting the sling to better cover the baby and attempting to stand. "Is there just the four of you?"

Brice lunged forward, as though he expected her to fall face first.

Moe, apparently thinking the same thing, nearly tripped over his boss in his headlong rush.

"Now you jest rest there, missy. These cowboys know how to pull their weight."

She hesitated.

Brice grinned. "He's a bossy old cuss. Better do what he says."

Moe made a colorful remark, then apologized for speaking so in front of a lady and baby.

Brice washed his hands and dished up five bowls of stew— or soup, rather—and set them on the table. He didn't know where these protective, coddling instincts had come from, and he wasn't sure he liked the feeling.

But one glance at the baby sleeping like an angel in Madison's arms made him go all soft in the head. The look of love on her face as she gazed down at her daughter simply arrested him, made him forget what he was doing until the heat from the soup bowl singed his fingers.

He wondered what it would be like to have someone look at him like that. And he wondered where that particular thought had come from.

"Eat," he ordered softly.

She gave him a sheepish smile. "So you can see if I keel over from the disaster?"

"I'm more worried about you keeling over from exhaustion than the food."

He sat down and took a bite. The vegetables were overcooked, the potatoes mushy, and the meat undercooked. Those lumps floating on top weren't dumplings; they were clumps of flour. But it was hot and chased away the chill of the day. "Not bad," he said.

"That's sweet of you to say, even though you're lying through your teeth."

"Shame on you. Cowboys never lie. It's in the code."

Maddie smiled, wishing she had the energy to just sit here and watch him. Oh, he was a fine specimen of a man.

And he was her employer, she reminded herself. Not some beefcake pinup to drool over. And if he found out she was basically on the run, that she was using the cover of this job as a hideout, he'd probably pack her up and ship her off with the UPS guy.

He'd taken on her and the unexpected baby with grace—albeit grudgingly—but that didn't mean he'd stand still for the rest of her personal baggage being dumped at his doorstep.

Just thinking about the whole mess made her insides churn, and she looked away.

The other two cowboys, along with Moe, tiptoed to the table and sat down, each sneaking a peek at the baby on their way.

The red-haired one, Dan, dropped his fork. It pinged loudly against the tile floor. The men froze, and Moe shot the ex-rodeo rider a scowl. "Shhh! You'll wake the young'un," he whispered in his gruff, gravelly voice.

Randy, young and focused solely on the meal before him—flour lumps and all—slurped soup from his spoon, earning himself the focus of Moe's censure. "Don't you got a lick of manners, boy? Yer in the company of women and children."

"Child. Singular," Dan mumbled.

"Apologies, ma'am," Randy murmured.

"It's okay," Madison said. "Y'all don't need to whisper."

Brice laid down his fork. "Is she sleeping in longer stretches yet?"

"Just catnaps."

"Looks like you could use one yourself."

His voice was soft and full of compassion—more like a lover's than an employer's. She glanced away. "I'm fine."

"You're practically falling asleep in your dinner."

"More coffee, Miss Maddie?"

"No, thank you, Moe." The older man was trying to be nonchalant, bless his heart, but she'd seen him discreetly pass his bowl under the table for Jax.

Thinking to get a head start on the dishes, she reached for the empty bread plate. It would take the better part of the night to set the kitchen to rights. Thank goodness the sling allowed her to operate with her hands free and still hold the baby. Now if only Abbe would cooperate and sleep.

Brice covered her hand with his. "Leave the dishes, sunshine. You're in no shape to do any more tonight."

Dan stood. "Boss's right. Besides, I'm on dish duty. Randy's in charge of drying and trash hauling."

Randy looked up in bewilderment. Moe took the opportunity to snatch his bowl right out from under his nose.

"No, really," Madison objected, then nearly melted into a puddle when Brice placed a finger over her lips. Her gaze snapped up to his. Fatigue pulled at the corners of his eyes. Not only was *she* worn-out, she was wearing Brice out too! And he was paying her for the privilege. Something was terribly wrong with this picture.

She was supposed to be proving that she was an asset, not a hindrance. And she seriously doubted that Dan and Randy normally did the dishes.

"Why don't you go on to bed and let me take the baby for a while."

Oh, what she wouldn't give for just five minutes of blissful sleep. "Brice, I came here to do a job—"

"Which makes me your boss. I'll rephrase. Get some sleep, sunshine. That's an order." He eased the sling from around her neck and carefully lifted the baby.

Three sets of hands shot out as though to help.

Brice scowled. "For crying out loud, you'd think I was going to drop her or something."

Moe scowled right back. "Well, gol-dang it, watch the head!"

"I know what I'm doing."

Dan and Randy moved closer. "She sure is a little thing," Randy commented.

"'Course she's little. She's hardly a week old. Now step back and give the boss some breathin' room."

Randy shrugged. "Looks like she could'a cooked a little longer, if you ask me."

"Nobody asked ya."

Though dead on her feet, Madison smothered a giggle at the sight of the four cowboys hovering, practically tripping over one another in an effort to help.

But the sight that arrested her the most, that made her heart swell, was of Brice. So tall and sturdy, the epitome of masculinity, holding her tiny baby in his arms, gazing at the infant as though she were his very own miracle.

He would make a great father.

Had she done Abbe a disservice by choosing to bring her into this world fatherless?

Just then Brice looked up. "Go," he said softly. "We've got everything under control."

"You sure?"

"Look, it's no big deal. Call it a bonus."

She rolled her eyes. "You're skeptical about me even working here in the first place—for that matter, I've yet to *do* any work—"

"You cooked."

"Worthwhile work, then." She dared him to spout platitudes

over that pitiful dinner. Even the dog had declined more after only a few bites. "And now you're handing out bonuses?"

He shrugged. "An early bonus in good faith, then. Besides, I'll be up for a while. Take the offer, sunshine. Abigail's asleep—I can't get in too much trouble. And if I do, I'll come get you."

She took him up on his offer. Her body ached in places she didn't know it could ache, and she was so tired she was dizzy.

But the minute her head hit the pillow, she knew that sleep wouldn't come. Her arms felt empty without Abbe in them. And she wasn't used to foisting her responsibilities off on others—namely Brice.

The threat of the Covingtons finding her, of Abbe being snatched away from her, was constantly on her mind. And that made her feel out of control.

After tossing and turning for what seemed like hours, Maddie finally got up. As she made her way down the hallway, she could hear Abbe fussing and Brice's deep soothing voice.

Soothing, but frazzled.

A cheery fire burned in the brick fireplace, the wood snapping and popping, casting an orange glow over the shadowy room. Brice paced the circumference of the braided rug, jiggling the baby, keeping up a constant stream of nonsensical conversation. He alternately begged, bribed and promised the moon, if only the infant would settle down.

It melted her heart to see this rugged cowboy holding her baby and blundering through Infant Trial and Error 101.

He'd removed his boots, and in sock feet—without the added two-inch boot heels—the hem of his pants dragged the floor. Someone really ought to put a hem in those things.

The receiving blanket, which before had been wrapped securely around the baby, was now half on and half off the infant, the thermal material trailing over Brice's arm. One of Abbe's tiny bare feet peeked out. Her little arms waved in obvious agitation, her fist colliding with the silk bandana he wore around his neck.

"Come on, princess," he said softly, his tone harried. "I've walked clear to Texas and back. What's the fuss? You didn't like the scenery?"

Maddie grinned and moved into the room. "Want me to take over?"

He jumped and whipped around. "Sheesh. Don't sneak up on me like that. I thought you were asleep."

She reached out to take her daughter. "I couldn't sleep."

The transfer was a little awkward. His fingers brushed her breasts; it couldn't be helped. There was nothing sexual about the touch, but she reacted nonetheless.

"I think she might be hungry," he said, making an effort to right the blanket, then giving up.

"Mmm, she's always hungry. If you could lay the blanket down over there on the sofa, I'll rewrap her."

He did as she asked. "She's such a wiggle-worm. I've already wrapped her up three times, but she keeps getting loose."

Maddie chuckled. "Do you suppose that's a sign she'll be a holy terror when she learns to do more than kick with these legs?" It struck her that they were discussing the baby as though she belonged to the two of them, as though looking down the road six months from now would find them still together—like a real family.

But Maddie couldn't plan six months from now. She could only take each day as it came, only concentrate on keeping her baby daughter safe.

"Don't ask me," Brice answered. "I've never been around babies before."

"I'm surprised. You're a natural."

He shrugged, moved to the window and pushed it open another fraction of an inch, then picked up the fireplace poker and added another log to the grate.

"Why do you do that?"

He looked at her. "Do what?"

"Open the windows when it's freezing outside."

"Habit."

He poked at the fire, and she waited to see if he'd say more.

When he glanced at her and caught her stare, he shrugged. "I fell down a well when I was a kid. Since then I'm not crazy about closed in spaces. An open window gives me the illusion of escape, I suppose."

"How awful for you."

"It was a long time ago."

"How long were you in it?"

"About five hours."

"Dear heaven, couldn't they find you?"

"They didn't know I was missing. My father and Moe were out riding fence. Dad figured my mother was watching over me. None of us had any idea that was the day she'd chosen to pack her bags and disappear."

"Oh, Brice." She started to move toward him, then thought better of it when she saw his shoulders stiffen, saw him turn his back on her. A stinging rush swept her when he shut her out. She should be used to that. She'd had plenty of experience with being ignored, looked through.

"Like I said, it was a long time ago. No big deal."

He obviously didn't accept comforting easily. And Abbe was working herself into a righteous snit, making her best effort to dislodge—once more—the tightly wrapped receiving blanket.

Brice ran his hand over the back of his neck. He was beat. And Madison didn't look much better. Nobody had ever asked him about the habit of open windows—or if they had, he hadn't answered. So what had possessed him to impart that little quirk to her? To blurt out the sordid details of his past.

He'd seen the compassion in her tired blue eyes, and something else. He couldn't abide pity, so he'd shut her out. He hadn't expected her reaction to his abruptness, the visible wince, the chin that inched up so subtly, the almost-tangible way she drew a protective coat over her emotions.

Hell on fire, she made him want to pick her up and wrap her in a blanket of protection, much like he'd tried to wrap the baby in the receiving blanket. Why did he keep getting the feeling that she *needed* his protection? That there were hidden secrets she held deep inside?

What was she running from? And where was Abbe's father? Were the answers one and the same?

Her hair fell forward as she leaned over the baby, cuddling, soothing—to no avail.

"Suppose you should try feeding her?" He stood next to her now, so close he could smell the shampoo of her hair. He saw the wariness on her face, the hesitation.

Idiot, he chided himself. Of course she would feed the baby. But she was uncomfortable nursing in front of him. And if the truth be told, so was he—even though he'd caught her at it several times, usually when he slipped into his bedroom to retrieve clothes or toiletries. They'd both ended up red-faced like a couple of preteens caught in their underwear.

She nodded, still hesitating.

"I'll...uh, go in the other room if it'll make you more comfortable," he offered, though he hated to leave her all alone, felt like a crummy host.

"Brice, this is your home, for heaven's sake. You don't have to go." She sat on the couch, picked up a crocheted afghan and draped it over her shoulder. "Women do this nursing stuff all the time. I'll admit, I'm having a little trouble adjusting." She shifted the baby, fumbled with her shirt.

Even though she was completely covered, he saw her struggle, had an urge to go help.

Hell. He turned toward the fire, as much to give her some privacy as to get himself under control. There was just something profoundly sensual about a woman nursing a baby. He wanted to watch, to hold her in his arms, to share the awe.

Man alive, he was losing it.

And getting in way too deep, way too soon.

That spelled danger.

He turned slowly, saw the skin pulled tight at the corners of her eyes as though she were in pain.

"You okay?"

"It'll pass in a minute." She winced.

He took a step forward. "What will pass?"

"Well...when I...when Abbe, uh, eats, it hurts."

"Is it supposed to?"

"How should I know? I've never nursed a baby before. Maybe it's just me. I've never heard anybody else complaining of feeling like stinging hot needles were piercing them."

"Maybe I should call Nancy. Ask her advice."

The nurse, Maddie thought. Why hadn't she thought to do that? Because she wasn't used to asking advice. She was used to going it alone.

"I'm taking up enough of your time already. Why don't you leave the number for me, and I'll call."

He nodded. "I'll put it by the phone in the kitchen. Doc will probably want to come out and have a look at the two of you, anyway. And until he does, I don't want you standing in the kitchen attempting to cook for us."

She grinned. "The stew was pretty bad, huh?"

"No."

She arched a brow.

"Well, you're operating under a handicap."

Major handicap, given the fact that she'd never cooked from scratch in her life. Tomorrow she'd see if there was a cookbook in residence. "I'll do better next time."

"I'm sure you will. But *not* until Doc gives the go-ahead. Understand?"

"We'll see."

"No, we won't. I mean it, sunshine. No KP till Doc says so."

"Honestly, Brice. Women have had babies since the beginning of time and not interrupted their duties."

"Maybe so, but none that I'd seen firsthand. I was there, remember? Hell, I think I was in more pain than you, during that birth."

She remembered. And the thought made her face heat. It was one thing to have a doctor looking, during such an inelegant experience, and quite another for it to be a handsome cowboy.

A cowboy who made her heart go into overdrive by just walking into a room. Especially wearing chaps.

Abbe had fallen asleep, and Madison couldn't bring herself to wake her and try to get her to nurse on the other breast. Which meant that she probably wouldn't sleep more than a half-hour stretch.

"Speaking of pain, I think my eyeballs are gonna fall out of my head. We should probably both get some sleep." She struggled to get up off the couch. Brice moved across the room and helped her up. He was so gallant. She wasn't used to someone, anyone, being so solicitous of her needs.

"Thank you."

He walked with her to his bedroom door. "Let me just grab a change of clothes. That way I won't wake you in the morning."

"I feel bad about taking your room. I'll move my stuff tomorrow."

"No. Just stay put. I'm fine in the guest room."

After he retrieved his clothes, she listened for him to close the door of the guest room. Instead, she heard him moving around in the room next to hers—obviously setting up the crib.

Dear Lord, where did the man get his stamina? He'd be up again before dawn, out in the cold, taking care of his ranch. And instead of getting much-needed sleep, he was assembling a nursery for her baby.

A special man. A very special man.

She'd make that call to the doctor first thing. Because healed or not, dead on her feet or not, she was going to pull her weight around here.

And try not to let it feel too much like home. She was only here by the grace of his kindness. She had to make sure she did her job—treated it like a job.

And that included forgetting erotic thoughts about her sexy boss.

Chapter Five

Nancy Adams came out the next morning to check on Maddie and Abbe. Doc had been called away on another emergency, and Maddie was just as glad. She could use another woman to talk to.

"I can't believe how my strength is zapped."

"Understandable. Honey, you've just had a baby."

"Still, I must be doing something wrong. She doesn't sleep more than twenty minutes or so at a stretch, and she constantly wants to nurse." She hesitated, then asked away. "Nursing is painful. It seems I'm not very good at it."

"Lets have a look, shall we?"

Despite Nancy's ability to put her at ease, Maddie still felt uncomfortable with these personal details. She felt heat stain her face and looked away as Nancy gently probed.

"Are you nursing on both sides?"

"Trying to, though I keep forgetting which one I left off on."

"A safety pin in your bra will fix that. But you've got bigger problems here."

"What?" She didn't like the sound of those words.

"You're running a fever, and there's infection in your breasts. Aside from lack of sleep, that's a big part of your low-level energy."

"Does that mean I have to stop nursing?"

"Well, no. If you're adamant about continuing, it's not out

of the question. I can start you on a mild antibiotic that won't hurt your daughter. But sometimes, in unfamiliar surroundings, under stress, your milk won't flow adequately. That could account for the baby not sleeping. She's not getting enough to eat."

"But I feel like a swollen dairy cow. How can it be that I don't have enough to nourish her?"

"It just happens sometimes. And I'm sure it makes it difficult living in this house with all these cowboys."

"Most of the men stay in the bunkhouse." Just Brice was here. And he did keep her off balance.

"But they come in and out, I'm sure. Which can get uncomfortable if you're in the middle of a feeding."

Maddie smiled. "Not just for me. They never seem to know where to look."

"Or not to look?" They shared a laugh.

"Try warm towels to encourage the milk flow, plus it'll be soothing. I'll leave a breast pump with you, and a supply of antibiotics. I'll also give you samples of formula so you can supplement with bottles, see if that helps things, if the baby will sleep longer stretches. That'll give you the best indication of whether or not she's getting enough to eat."

Maddie felt like a total failure. "How can I screw up something so simple, so natural, as breast feeding?" She hadn't meant to voice the words, but there they were. And formula wasn't an expense she'd counted on.

Nancy placed a comforting hand on Maddie's shoulder. "Don't beat yourself up over this. Breast milk does give babies a good start, but formulas are the next best thing. There's no law that says you *have* to breast feed, and there's no shame in choosing not to. Besides, look at the pros of opting for the bottle. Somebody else can get up in the middle of the night."

"Not in my case."

"Oh? What about Brice? Anyone can see he's absolutely silly over this baby."

"But she's my responsibility."

Nancy gave a slight frown at the fierceness of the statement. "Well, whatever you decide. In the meantime, we ought to get the paperwork filled out for the birth certificate."

Panic winged out of nowhere. Paperwork was traceable. She needed to give this some thought. "Can I ask you a question?"

"Sure, honey."

How in the world would she phrase this? After several minutes of silence, she finally just dived right in.

"Am I required to put my last name on the birth certificate?"

"Yes," Nancy said slowly. "That's standard... Oh, I see, you want to give the child her father's name? Well that will be fine. You just list your name as mother, his under father, and assign his name behind Abigail's."

Tough to do when she'd intended to list father as "unknown."

"Have you contacted the father?" Nancy asked softly, obviously couching the words so it wouldn't appear as though she were prying—or judging.

Maddie shook her head. At least in this she could give the truth. "He's deceased."

"Oh, I am sorry. Of course you'd want his legacy to live on through his daughter."

Nancy had no way of knowing that those words were the wrong ones to say, that they tapped right into her nightmare. But she'd given herself an opening to stall.

"We weren't exactly...together." Major understatement. "Could you just leave the papers here with me? Give me some time to think it over, decide which way I want to go?"

"Of course dear. George likes to get this done right away, and in the hospital it's mandatory before you leave. But we can fudge a bit since you delivered at home. I'll just leave this with you. You can sign in the appropriate places, write the other information on a separate piece of paper, and I'll type it in and get it filed with the state."

"Thank you. And thank you for coming out to check on us."

"No problem. That's my job. That it's for a new neighbor makes it doubly fun. I'm glad you're here on the Flying D. Brice needs a woman around."

"Oh, I'm not…I mean, I'm only working for him."

Nancy smiled and patted her on the shoulder again. "Of course, dear." Her tone held undercurrents that Maddie didn't want to speculate on. "Try the breast pump. Warm towels beforehand. Though don't get discouraged if it doesn't work. Most of my new moms despise the things, usually settle for the premix formula."

"I'll give it a good shot."

"That's all you can do. In the meantime, take it easy, go at your own pace, and resume any activities you feel up to. Except intercourse. You'll want to wait another week or so if you've a mind to indulge."

"I'm not of a mind…" Good heavens, where had the nurse gotten an idea like that? And… "Did you say a *week?* Singular? I thought the time period was six weeks. Not that I'm going to," she clarified hastily. "Or that there's any possibility."

Nancy gave another one of those enigmatic smiles. "All women heal at different rates. Some would just as soon wait a year, and some are ready and willing in a couple of weeks, claim their hormones have gone loco. The human body's a gloriously resilient thing. Just don't tell a *man* that."

Maddie couldn't help but smile back. "In the interest of the sisterhood, my lips are sealed."

Nancy laughed again. "Oh, I do like you, Madison Carlyle. Call if you need anything, or just want to talk. It doesn't have to involve a medical question. And if you decide you want to go the formula route, give a call over to Letty Springer's market in town. Brice has the number. They'll even send someone out to deliver."

Dear heaven, the Flying D was going to get a reputation for odd and frequent deliveries.

MADDIE TOOK the antibiotics and fed Abbe a bottle of the formula Nancy had left. The traitorous little baby had gulped it down and was now sleeping like an angel. It made her feel awful that she'd actually been starving her child. Next she'd tried the pump. It had taken nearly an hour to suck out half an ounce.

She felt swollen and feverish and disheartened. She would have loved to lie down and take a nap, but decided instead to familiarize herself with Brice's accounting practices.

It was a nightmare. He had a state-of-the-art computer, but when she tried to call up files, there were no documents. How in the world did he run this huge operation with such dismal accounting practices.

At least this was something she was good at, and she dived right in, methodically sorting through the records. More than one client had dumped a shoebox full of receipts on her desk, expecting her to make sense out of it. Brice's accounts were the equivalent of that type of client.

A challenge. Just like the man himself.

The more she delved into his paperwork, the more surprised she was.

He was very successful. And very wealthy.

And he shopped at JCPenney—a lot.

She checked the depreciation schedule on his previous year's taxes, stunned at the amount of equipment and number of vehicles he owned.

And he had an airplane, a single-engine Cessna.

Maddie felt her fingers itch. She loved flying, had taken lessons and gotten her own pilot's license six years ago. At the time, she'd been dating a pilot and shared flight time on his plane. In hindsight, the draw of that particular relationship for her had been his plane. When they broke up, the friendship had dissolved—along with the agreement of shared air time. And she missed it. The flying, not the man.

She also stumbled on another interesting bit of information. Brice had been married. He'd been writing alimony checks to a Sharon DeWitt up until a year ago.

For some reason that she couldn't pinpoint, it bothered her that he'd been married, that another woman had lived with him here, shared intimacies over the breakfast table, had ridden with him across his land, flown with him in his plane, made love with him…admired his butt in those sexy-as-sin chaps.

Caught up in her musing, she nearly bolted out of the chair when Brice walked into the room.

"I was just checking your books." Her cheeks flamed, and she felt like a thief caught with her hand in the till—even though he'd given her permission to have a go at the books. As a CPA, she knew intimate details about her clients' lives; occasionally she raised an eyebrow or gave a chuckle, but she'd never jolted like this, never felt as though she were invading a client's privacy.

She took a breath, steadied her nerves.

"I see you were married." It came out as an accusation, and she could have just died.

"Ancient history."

"Not too ancient. You paid pretty hefty alimony." She tried to sound businesslike, which was difficult with him watching her so. He looked tired, but oh, so enticing. She noticed that his hat did indeed brush the top of the doorjamb as she'd expected it would. She cleared her throat. "No checks recently, though."

"Those ended when Sharon remarried. She's expecting a baby."

"Oh. Is that a good thing? I mean, are you okay with it?" Was he still carrying a torch for his ex-wife? And why in the world should that matter?

"Sure. She always wanted kids."

Her brows rose. "And you didn't?"

"Couldn't." He moved into the room, his loose-hipped stride mesmerizing her.

"Sorry." She shouldn't have pried. But when he stopped in front of the desk, she was eye level with his silver belt buckle—and realized that chaps, from a front view, were even more erotic than from the back. Buckled low on his hips, with ties going between his legs, they formed a frame on his anatomy that no "good" girl should be staring at.

Well, she'd never considered herself a good girl.

Still, her hormones gave a healthy, glad leap, and though she told herself it wasn't polite to pry, her brain and mouth couldn't seem to get their signals straight.

"How long were you married?" She saw amusement in his eyes and waved a hand in a gesture of apology. "Never mind. I'm certain it's none of my business."

He perched a hip on the corner of the desk. "Two years and one winter."

She frowned and drummed her fingers on the desk, completely forgetting that she'd just decided not to pry. "That's an odd way of answering."

"Winters out here are tough. Sharon was a city girl." His tone held a slight hint of accusation. "She needed malls and people, fine dining—that kind of stuff."

"But you've got a plane." She said it as though that would solve everything. "Aren't those places easily accessible by air?"

"Sharon wasn't crazy about flying. Actually, she hated it, was scared silly."

Maddie couldn't imagine such a thing. And being a pilot herself—though she hadn't flown in ages—she knew what it felt like if the trust level of your passenger was missing.

"Besides," Brice went on. "Ranching's a seven-day-a-week job, it isn't something you put on hold to go gallivanting to the nearest mall five hundred miles away. I didn't have the time to fly her to the city every weekend."

"Oh." Just like he didn't have the time to be checking on her and Abbe every few hours—day and night—she thought.

Brice shifted against the desk, removed his hat and toyed with the brim. Talking about the past made him uncomfortable. Frankly, he didn't even know why he was volunteering the information—except for the fact that his life was basically laid out for her in the pages of his ranch records.

"How's the bookkeeping going? Making any headway?"

"I'm just getting my feet wet. You've got a great computer here. Why haven't you used it?"

"I haven't the slightest clue how, and I don't really want to."

"Then why'd you buy it?"

"My ex bought it."

"Well, I'll teach you how to use it. I'm good at this kind of stuff. And once you get the hang of it, you'll wonder how you ever got along without it."

"I doubt it. Just don't do away with my manual system." When she left—and he was sure she would—he didn't want some damned machine holding his records hostage.

"Okay. I'll design two sets of books, one by hand and the other on the computer. But I'm betting you'll like what the computer can do."

"We'll see." He ran his fingers over the corded band of his hat, then set it aside on the desk. "I talked to Leonard today. Your car's ready."

"Oh, good," she said absently, looking thoroughly in her element as she scanned entries in his journals. "What was wrong with it?"

"Burned electrical wire." He waited a couple of seconds, watched the way she drummed her fingers against the desk. He noticed that she did that a lot. Like a nervous habit. "So, when you're up to it you're free to leave."

He saw the instant panic, saw her fingers still, close into a fist, her knuckles going white.

"It'll take a while to straighten out the books."

"Don't let that stop you from getting on with your life. The old way has worked fine for me all these years."

She stood, paced. "But you said it needed streamlining. Plus you hired me to cook—"

"Madison."

"And you bought the baby furniture." She turned, stepped close, nearly fitting herself between his widely spread knees.

"You can't fire me so soon. You've got to give me a chance to prove myself."

Her hands were fisted in his shirtfront, her lips a breath away from his. Desire, swift and fierce, caught him by surprise.

"I'm not firing you."

"You're not?"

She moved closer, scorching him with her heat when the tips of her breasts brushed his chest. She was wearing her contact lenses today; he could see the discs floating over her light blue irises. Something passed between them: a silent communication, an invisible, sultry dance that a man learned to recognize at puberty.

He had no idea how it had happened. One minute she was strung tighter than a steel post, then the next, her features had softened, her breath quickened. She licked her lips, focused her gaze on his mouth.

He nearly swallowed his tongue.

"I just said…" He couldn't help it. He had to touch her. Reaching out, he tucked a stray strand of blond hair behind her ear. Her eyes went even wider, and damn it, he had an irrational urge to taste her.

"Said what?" Her voice was soft, breathy.

He needed to get out of here before he did something he'd regret. "Never mind. I've got to get back to work." He eased her away from him and stood, nearly groaning when their thighs brushed, pressed for an instant.

She stepped back to give him room. Reluctantly, it seemed.

Man alive, this woman spelled trouble. For a minute there, he'd thought she intended to seduce him into letting her stay. And with Madison, he didn't think it was a conscious act of calculation; it was more an act of desperation.

There was something deeper to the panic he keep seeing in her eyes. He wanted to know what it was.

But right now wasn't a good time. For self-preservation, he had to put some distance between them.

Because the longer she stayed, the deeper he got. Already he found himself making excuses to come back to the house, anxious to see Madison and the baby.

And that was a dangerous habit to get hooked on.

Especially now that he was also looking for any excuse under the sun to kiss her.

And resisting those excuses with Herculean effort.

BRICE ADJUSTED the bandanna around his neck and tugged his hat lower on his forehead. It had snowed off and on for the past two days. A fresh power of white covered the ground and the wind blew like a banshee. He tried to tell himself that the wind was a good thing; it cleared patches of ground so the cattle could forage. Unlike other animals, cows wouldn't paw and root through the snow to find grass, which would amount to a huge loss of beef if a rancher didn't keep a close eye.

Still, Mother Nature was fickle. The winds could die off as quickly as they'd blown in. It wouldn't be safe to wait much longer before they moved the rest of the herd to a lower section.

And that, of course, would mean spending a night away from the ranch.

Brice's reluctance to carry on with his work disgusted him.

Damn it, Madison Carlyle was an employee. He had no business worrying about her and her little baby, had no business itching to hold them both, wanting to stick close to home in case— In case what? he wondered, aggravated with himself.

He hefted the final bale of hay and tossed it over the bed of the truck.

"That should do it for a while," he said to Dan. "I'll clear the road on the way in." He was driving the pickup with the snowplow attached to the front. The engine was running with the heater going full force. Still, his bones ached from the cold. "There's a line down in the East section."

"Randy's already on it. I'll head that way and give him a hand." The red-haired ranch hand vaulted over the side of the pickup, wincing slightly as his bum leg tried to buckle beneath him. Tough and wiry, never once did he complain.

Brice shut the tailgate of the truck and tugged his hat lower against the wind. Dan stepped closer, pitched his voice so it wouldn't carry any farther than the two of them.

"You might want to take Moe with you, boss. He's got no business being out in this nasty cold, and he's too damned prideful to quit."

Brice nodded. "I'd planned to." He raised his voice against the wind. "Come on, Bertelli. If I'm gonna plow us a path, I'll need an extra set of eyes peeled for downed fences."

Moe's pride shot up quicker than a cat's back. "You got better eyes than a buzzard sightin' a carcass, and you know it, boy."

"Maybe so, but if I run us in a ditch trying to do two things at once, I won't be fit company for a good long time."

"Yeah," Dan said. "And the rest of us'll pay."

Moe shot Dan a squinty-eyed look, then glanced back at Brice. "You ain't been fit company in a coon's age, and yer impertinent to boot." Grumbling, he yanked open the passenger door of the truck. "You gonna stand there all day grinning like a 'possum, or we gonna get?"

Brice made an effort to subdue his laughter. He was crazy about this old man and wouldn't deliberately hurt Moe's pride for the world. "I imagine we'll get," he said, imitating the other man's words.

The snow wasn't sticking too bad. As he scraped the way with the front plow, he activated the dump, welded beneath the bed of the truck that dispensed salt crystals.

He stopped twice to pound stakes against barbwire sections that were sagging from the wind and weight of the snow, and by the time they neared the barn, he felt like a block of ice.

"Looks like we got comp'ny," Moe said.

Brice saw the late-model Dodge truck with a horse trailer

hitched to the back, saw the man hunched against the wind, standing on the front veranda as though he'd knocked but hadn't gotten an answer.

Where was Madison? Out here if a stranger came calling, it was neighborly to let him in to warm up.

His gut clenched and his senses went on alert. Was something wrong with her? With the baby? Disaster scenarios flitted one after the other through his mind. He pulled right up to the front door, left the truck running. "Take it to the shed for me," he said to Moe and opened the door. "I'll see what's up."

The guy was young, appeared to be a drifter. Nice wheels, though. "Help you with something?"

The man stuck out his gloved hand. "Name's Mike Collier. Came to inquire about work."

Brice had a pretty full staff as it was for this time of year. Then again, there was the herd of Angus he'd planned to move. He hated to turn away a man in need. He had the biggest spread north of the Nebraska divide and was in a better position than his neighbors to take on an added expense.

Besides, an extra man might be more of an incentive for Moe to stick closer to the homestead.

"You from around these parts?"

"Up Montana way. I'm a hard worker. Don't mind the cold."

Brice knew he ought to ask a few more questions, but at the moment he was anxious to find out why Madison wasn't answering the door.

"Fine then." He named a salary, inclined his head toward the bunkhouse. "Go ahead and stow your gear. Moe Bertelli will fill you in on the operation."

"Much obliged, sir."

"DeWitt," Brice corrected. "Brice DeWitt."

The drifter nodded and went to retrieve is belongings.

Brice twisted the front doorknob and frowned when he found it locked. His heart pumped harder. He rarely locked the door. No one did around these parts.

Tugging his glove off with his teeth, he fished for the spare key wedged behind the wood shutter decorating the window.

The curtain fluttered, then the door swung open.

He stepped in, shut the door behind him and focused on Madison. She looked fragile and pale, as though her nerves were a calf's breath away from shattering. Her blue eyes held the barest hint of panic.

Feeling on the verge of panic himself, he quickly scanned the room for signs of injury or anything else amiss. A cheery fire crackled in the hearth. The magazines were stacked neatly on the maple table and the room smelled of lemon polish and pine logs.

He made it to her side in three strides, tipped up her chin. "What is it?"

"Nothing."

He frowned. "Don't hand me that. You look like you've just come face-to-face with a starving mountain lion. Why didn't you answer the door? I thought something had happened to you or the baby."

She turned away from him, moved to the fireplace, held her hands out for warmth. He saw the fine trembling in her fingers.

It was time he got some answers.

He rested his hands on her shoulders, turned her to face him. Snow dripped from the brim of his hat, melted on the shoulders of his jacket.

"Talk to me, sunshine. You're scared of something. Maybe I can help."

"You have," she said quietly. "You gave me a job."

That was debatable, but he set the thought aside. "Are you in trouble?"

She closed her eyes, stepped back. "Who was the man at the door?"

"A drifter looking for work."

"Are you sure?"

"He said so. That's good enough for me." He peeled off his coat, tossed it along with his hat and gloves onto a recliner chair. "You told me that there wasn't a Mr. Carlyle, so I imagine I'm barking up the wrong tree if I'm drawing parallels of association between you and Mike Collier?"

"Who?"

"The guy I just hired."

"You mean you hired him in a matter of minutes? Just like that without finding out anything about him?" She wrapped her arms around her middle, gave a quick glance down the hall, as though she had a desperate need to check on her baby. She hadn't responded to his question, but he had his answer. She didn't know Mike Collier. But she was definitely spooked.

He raised a brow. "I hired you pretty much the same way—sight unseen."

"Yes. And just look what you got for your trouble."

He didn't think she'd meant to say that. And though he still had doubts about her suitability as a cook and housekeeper, some mushy spot deep inside him didn't want to classify her as a mistake.

Which showed very poor judgment on his part.

"I should go check on Abbe."

He snagged her arm, held her still. "She's not crying. Leave her be." He urged her down on the couch, spread an afghan over her lap. Her sweatpants were thin and she was shivering.

"Talk to me, Madison. You're not a cook, yet you go into a tailspin when I suggest that the Flying D isn't really the place for you—"

"I *can* cook," she argued.

"I'm sure you can. But it's not a profession that utilizes your qualifications. It's also something you're not crazy about doing. So that gets me to wondering why you would answer my ad in the first place. Why you're willing to seduce me into letting you stay—"

"I did not!"

"Why you panic when a drifter shows up," he finished, ignoring her denial. "Who are you, Madison Carlyle? And what are you hiding from?"

Chapter Six

Madison had hoped to bluff her way onto the ranch, to do a good job—because she always excelled at whatever task she took on—and to find safety.

She'd hoped this subject wouldn't come up.

But it had. She'd obviously lost her touch at hiding her emotions. Which was too bad; the stakes had never been this high before.

She picked at the fuzz on the deep green afghan, sighed. After all he'd done for her, Brice deserved answers.

Trusting others didn't come easily. This time, she had to chance it.

"I'm not sure where to start," she said at last, wishing he would sit down. His working attire was highly distracting.

He poked at the fire, then obliged her without even knowing it and sat on the edge of the chair closest to the hearth.

"Take your time. Start at the beginning or the middle. I'll try to keep up."

Her fingers drummed a silent beat against her thigh.

"I had my life all mapped out, a house that I loved, a successful business. It's been a struggle building a certain life-style. But I'd reached my goals." She smoothed her hair behind her ear, started to rub her eyes, then remembered her contact lenses at the last minute.

"I'm almost twenty-nine, and I wanted a child, wanted to

be a mother in the worst way. It was the right time for me. So I researched the process, saved my money."

"You…you *researched* it?" He sounded incredulous, looked a little stunned, as though he'd just swallowed a bug.

She laughed, surprised that she could, in light of the picture she was trying to paint for him. "Abbe is the product of artificial insemination," she clarified.

"Oh. Okay. I'm with you now—not that I understand." He raked a hand through his dark hair. "We do that with the cattle to ensure superior stock—but, why would a beautiful woman like you resort to those methods?"

"I'm not beautiful."

"Matter of opinion. Explain…if you don't mind."

Did she mind? There was discomfort with the disclosure, but it wasn't as difficult as she'd anticipated.

"It was the easiest and most logical means to my ends. I haven't dated anyone in a while, so there were no husband prospects on the horizon. According to my timetable, I wanted to be a mother by the time I turned thirty. Thus, my decision to choose a stranger-donor rather than conventional methods." She could have told him that the last thing she'd been looking for was a husband.

She remembered her father, who wasn't exactly the shining example of what a husband should be. He'd rarely paid her or her mother any attention.

The memories of a five-year-old, yearning for a family unit, for love, had been burned into her brain on a rainy day in Kentucky. The day her father had deserted their family without even a soft word or touch for the little girl who'd worshiped him, the little girl who'd tried desperately to cling, who would settle for a rough shove because at least that was contact.

"What about the kid?" Andrea Carlyle had shouted at his retreating back, standing on the sagging porch of their squalid two-room house. "How am I supposed to raise this kid with no money, you son of a bitch?"

Derk Carlyle had turned back, his eyes cold, never even

bothering to look at Madison, never even noticing the fat tears that rolled down her chubby cheeks. "You think I give a damn? She's probably not even mine. Give her over to the state for all I care."

The words had settled like a swarm of stinging bees on Madison's tiny heart. She'd stood right there on the condemned porch with its peeling paint and network of fire ants working away on a rotten tomato...and she'd wet her pants.

And the next day her mother had given her away.

"Madison?"

She started at Brice's voice and shook off the memory.

"I wanted Abbe more than my life. I won't give her up. And I won't let anyone take her from me."

"Easy, sunshine," he soothed, reaching out to her, yet not touching. "Is someone trying to take her?"

"Yes." Just admitting it out loud made her palms go damp and her stomach lurch. "My sperm donor was anonymous. I didn't want to know his name. And the records are supposed to be sealed and confidential. But there was a mix-up somehow... well, I suspect it had more to do with palms being greased. Money can buy most anything, including supposedly confidential information."

"Okay, I'm trying to keep up, but I've missed a step here."

"My sperm donor's name was Stephen Covington. He died in a skiing accident several months ago. His family is wealthy, and he was the last of their dynasty. His parents found records of him donating sperm—and now they want the product of that sperm, the only piece of their son they have left."

"That's ridiculous. They have no rights."

"I don't know whether they do or not. But they do have money—more than I can get ahold of—and they're very determined to fight for my baby...by fair means or foul."

He swore.

"Exactly. So I ran before they could serve legal papers, before the battle could begin. I won't give her up. That's why I need this job, Brice. No one knows I'm here. No one would think to look for me here—I hope. But I'm smart enough to realize the Covingtons will hire private investigators."

She stood, went to the window, looked out at the snow that was blowing even harder. She shivered.

"That's why I freaked when your drifter showed up. He could just as easily be a hired detective as a ranch hand."

Brice noticed the rigid length of her spine. It was all falling into place now. Her strange reaction when Doc had suggested they publicize her baby as the first one born in the new year; her panic when he suggested she wasn't right for the job; her reluctance to fill out the birth certificate forms; the protective, fierce way she cuddled her baby.

Ah, hell. He didn't want to get involved. Because he had a tendency to care too much, to get in too deep.

And his heart invariably suffered.

Still, he went to her, moved right across the room and placed his hands gently on her tense shoulders.

"I shouldn't have bluffed about my qualifications for this position," she said softly, her gaze still fixed beyond the panes of the window. "I'd counted on this ranch as being my safe haven, counted on being able to lie low in hopes that the Covingtons wouldn't find me, or that they'd give up. I'm sorry," she whispered.

Oh, man. He felt his armor crack. He could see their reflections in the glass pane, a tiny woman with the weight of the world on her shoulders, and a rough, lonely cowboy who was too stupid to learn from past mistakes.

But how could he turn her away when she considered him her safe haven?

"I'll check out the new guy," he said at last. "I'm a little territorial over that baby myself. I won't let anything happen to her."

She turned then, and the gratitude shining in her blue eyes slammed into him like a swift kick of a wild mustang.

And just that quickly, gratitude turned into something else, something elemental and earthy and irresistible.

His thumbs brushed the delicate column of her neck, sketched the curve of her jaw. So soft. So warm.

And he was a man in desperate need of warming.

Without thought, without apology or permission, his head lowered. At the first touch of their lips, he knew he'd made a huge error in judgment.

But the momentum was there, the need too strong. She tasted like his destiny—yet she couldn't *be* his destiny. She was running, hiding…temporary.

So many people had been temporary in his life.

But he couldn't help himself. He angled his head for better access, needing more, so much more, feeling his heart pump like a thoroughbred's in a flat-out run.

She opened her mouth to him, let him in to explore, gave a soft, sensuous moan that fueled the raging inferno inside him.

He shifted her, tasted, nibbled, heard the erotic catch of her breath, felt her fingers dig into his shoulders. Something damp penetrated both his shirt and his hazy consciousness.

He eased back, noticed the wetness on the front of her sweatshirt.

Reality slammed into him. Good God, this woman had just had a baby less than two weeks ago, and here he was so carried away, aching to take her to bed.

He felt like a louse.

"That probably shouldn't have happened." His voice sounded rough and splintery.

"Probably not. But it was very nice. Thank you."

He felt his hairline shift as his brows rose. Her simple honesty touched him. She didn't berate him for taking liberties, or duck her head in feminine coyness. She met his gaze straight on and *thanked* him.

She placed her palm against his chest, right over the dampness left from her milk-swollen breasts. He nearly snatched her to him again, regardless of the recent childbirth. But her next words stopped him cold.

"So, if my whereabouts haven't been discovered, and I promise to bone up on the cooking thing, can I stay?"

He stepped back so fast she nearly did a face plant on the carpet. "Is that what that kiss was about?"

She looked genuinely confused. And he got a bad feeling. Maybe he'd jumped the gun—which wouldn't be a first for him.

He knew the exact moment understanding dawned; he could see it in the snap of her eyes, the fisting of her palm.

"I could slug you for a question like that." Clearly seething, she took a step forward.

Prudent man that he was, he backed up a pace. "Madison—"

"How dare you. You parade around here at all hours of the day and night wearing those…those made-for-sin chaps." She waved a hand toward the offending garments in question. "You hold my baby daughter as though she's the most precious, priceless piece of china, anticipate our needs before we can even voice them…."

She poked him in the chest then.

He bit his cheek to stop the grin. He knew better.

"You ooze sex appeal in all that cowboy gear, sending my hormones into a tizzy—" she poked him again "—and then have the nerve to ask a crummy question like that?"

"Madison—?"

"I *wanted* to kiss you, you jerk!"

He captured her finger before she could do serious damage. "Madison?"

"What?"

Her chest rose and fell, distracting him.

"I'm sorry."

"And well you should be."

She seemed to realize the extent of what she'd said. Embarrassment caught up with her. She looked away.

He caught her chin, turned her back to face him. "So you think I'm sexy?" Why the hell was he baiting her?

"As if you don't already know exactly what you look like," she said with a hint of disgust. "It's more than a fortunate gene pool, though. It's what's inside you that's attractive. You're a special man."

He was stunned—and charmed. "I don't think I've ever met a woman as honest as you."

She gave an inelegant snort. "You call it honest to answer a job ad when you don't know the first thing about cooking unless it comes in a microwavable package?"

He felt a grin pulling at his mouth. "That bad?"

"Yes. But I'm a quick study and very teachable. With the aid of a cookbook, I can probably manage not to starve you—that is, if you're willing to give me a chance."

He wanted to give her more than a chance. But he had one more, vitally important question. "And if my newly hired ranch hand turns out to be a private eye, will you still be wanting that chance?"

She let out a weary breath, pulled her hand from his. "I'll still want it, yes. That doesn't mean I can let myself have it. I have to think of Abbe first."

In other words, she would leave.

And that was the rub. Sooner or later, private investigators or not, she *would* leave.

They all did eventually.

Where before his heart had felt light, it now sank like a stone in his chest. At least she was honest.

Her top priority was protecting her baby daughter.

His was protecting his heart.

And he had a really bad feeling that one of them was going to lose—most likely him.

He reached for his hat and coat. "I'll check out the new guy, find out if he's on the up-and-up." As he moved to the door, he felt her gaze on him.

And damned if he didn't feel self-conscious.

Never before had he been so aware of his protective gear and the way it was worn. Sexy-as-sin chaps?

Lord Almighty, the men would howl like crazed hyenas if they got wind of that description.

Snow crunched beneath his boots as he trudged to the barn. There was a break in the weather, but that didn't mean it would last. While it did, though, the guys up at the line camp where they were holding the herd would have it easier. Cows drifted with a storm, wandered, and rounding them up was a miserable job in frigid winds and blowing snow.

He passed the stockyards where the bulls and some of the weaker cattle were penned, then went into the barn, giving Samson an affectionate scratch.

Jax greeted him with a happy bark.

"Hey, boy, you keep disappearing on me." Jax woofed again and turned in a tight circle, and Brice knew the dog wanted him to follow. "Okay, I'm coming. Anxious to show off your pups, hmm?"

The familiar scents of straw and leather and horses surrounded him like an old friend. When they reached the stall where the border collie guarded her offspring, he understood Jax's anxiety.

The newly hired ranch hand was squatted in the corner, gently cradling one of the puppies.

The man looked up without apology, steady nerves, as though there was nothing to hide. Brice didn't know what a private eye looked like, but this guy didn't fit the image. He had cowboy written all over him, from the angle of his hat, to the way he held himself, to the innate comfort in his surroundings.

"Did you get settled in all right?"

"Yeah. Bertelli filled me in. I figured if it was okay with you, I'd go on up to the line camp and pitch in. Seems that'd be the best place I'd be needed."

Pride was evident in Mike Collier's voice. He wasn't a loafer looking for a free ride.

"What spread did you say you came from?" Normally, Brice wouldn't have asked such a question, but Madison's panic made him bend his own personal code of behavior.

"The Circle C in Montana. Leon Stevers is the boss man if you want to check."

"No need." Brice recognized the name. For Madison's sake, he'd probably go ahead and give a call to Stevers, but he wouldn't insult Mike by saying so. "I imagine Sully and Luke would appreciate an extra hand up at the line camp." He took out a piece of paper, drew a simple map and handed it to Mike. "I'll radio ahead and tell Sully to expect you."

Mike nodded, placed the puppy back in its mother's warmth. "I appreciate the work."

"Happy to oblige. Let me show you the stock and you can pick a mount."

"I prefer my own, if it's all the same."

Brice had forgotten about the trailer that had been hitched to the Dodge. Another indication that this guy was exactly who he said he was. "Good enough. I'll set you up with a string of ponies and have you pack in a few supplies. Save me a trip. It'll probably be best if you wait until morning, get a fresh start."

Mike moved to the barn door, glanced up at the sky. "It's up to you, boss, but we've got a break in the weather right now. No telling what morning will bring."

"Suit yourself, then."

As Mike went to saddle his mount, Brice outfitted the pack ponies, wrestling with himself over whether or not he should call over to the Montana spread. There was a certain look about Mike Collier, a look that Brice recognized.

The man was a loner—a *lonely* man. And Brice knew about loneliness, saw a part of himself in this hired hand—and that bothered him.

Especially now that Madison and her little baby had burst into his life. He'd pretty much resigned himself to being alone.

Now he was starting to dream.

IN THE KITCHEN, Maddie was seriously beginning to question why babies didn't come equipped with removable batteries, or at least a disconnect button to turn off this crying.

She'd tried breast feeding again, and obviously it had been unsuccessful. Abbe continued to cry her little heart out.

"Oh, sweetie, Mommy's sorry. Here now. Hush. Please hush." She walk and jiggled and worried.

That's probably what the problem was. She was worried, stressed, and her emotions were transferring to the baby. Was Brice making any headway with finding out about his new ranch hand?

She was tempted to brave the freezing temperatures and hunt him down to ask.

But Abbe had other ideas. She was working herself into another snit.

And the spaghetti sauce was burning on the bottom of the skillet. She tried to put the baby in the infant seat, but she screamed louder.

The back door opened. Madison whirled around.

Moe Bertelli stopped dead in his tracks. "Didn't mean to scare ya."

"Sorry. It's a wonder I even heard you over Abbe's lungs. You might consider a pair of earplugs if you're going to stay."

"Naw." The older man hung up his hat. "A herd of bawlin' calves makes more ruckus than this little sweetheart. These old ears are used to it."

"In that case, here." Before Moe knew what was what, Maddie gently plopped Abbe in his arms. "Hold her for a minute so I can see if this spaghetti sauce can be salvaged."

"Well…" Moe sputtered, looking highly uncomfortable and stiff, then plopped down in a chair. "I'm dirtier than a buzzard feastin' on a carcass." His brow cleared, and his weathered face softened into a silly grin when the baby settled a bit. "Guess she don't mind a whiff of cow smell. See there? I got the touch."

Madison smiled. "My touch needs some work, apparently." She scraped the meat that was indeed stuck to the bottom of the pan, feeling out of sorts. She wished Brice would get in here and put her mind at ease about the new hired hand.

And she wished she could accomplish a decent meal without screwing it up, including feeding her own baby.

The baby snuffled, and Moe looked proud as a peacock that her cry wasn't sounding like life and death anymore. "She's just plum tuckered out, is all."

"You're doing fine, Moe. Let me just make up a couple of bottles and I'll take her."

"I don't mind spellin' you a bit. Fact, I think I'm gettin' the right of it." He stopped, frowned. "Did you say bottles? You weanin' her so soon?"

Madison bit her lip. "Nancy Adams said it might be best. I'm having some trouble in that area."

Moe's hazel eyes automatically snapped to Madison's breasts, then the tips of his ears turned bright red and he looked away. "Don't s'pose I need to be knowin' them details."

Oh, dear, she'd embarrassed him. She couldn't stop the bubble of laughter that welled. "I've really turned this place upside down, haven't I?"

"'Bout damn time if ya ask me. Pardon my cussin'."

Maddie wanted to ask what he meant about it being time, but Brice came in, bringing a burst of cold air with him. The steam from the bubbling spaghetti sauce fogged the kitchen window.

Brice glanced around at the homey scene—supper on the stove, Madison in sock feet, looking all soft and welcoming in a long green dress made of thermal cotton, baby bottles lining the counter top, Moe Bertelli holding the baby—

He did a double take, then grinned. The old man looked stiffer than a rooster's comb, but highly pleased with himself.

"Loafing, Bertelli?"

Moe muttered something crass, then apologized to both the baby and Madison. "The day you catch me loafin' is the day you find me pushin' up daisies." The baby wriggled and started in again on her crying. "Now see what ya done. Come in here bringin' the cold and disturbin' the peace. Best you get to washin' that barnyard off, cuz you're on next watch with the little girlie here."

Actually, Brice's palms fairly itched to hold Abbe. There was just something soft and soothing when that baby was in his arms—even if she was crying like a pitiful kitten.

But holding her reminded him of what he could never have.

Children of his own.

And Madison Carlyle.

"Last time I checked, I was still the boss around here." He decided who took what watch. "I could use a shower before supper if that's all right," he said to Madison.

"Humph," Moe muttered. "Thought you jest said you was the boss and here you go askin' permission."

Brice ignored his friend and left the kitchen before he did something stupid, like grabbing Madison and kissing that soft spot at the base of her neck where a tendril of blond hair clung.

"Brice?"

He turned, noticing she'd followed him out of the room. The shadows were back in her eyes—and something else he couldn't read. A hesitant determination that put him on the alert.

"Did you find out anything?"

About the new guy. "He's on the up-and-up. Just a drifter looking for work."

Her shoulders relaxed. And now she was looking at him as if somehow he was her salvation.

"After supper, can we talk?"

He wanted to say no. Anxiety came out of nowhere, emotions he didn't understand, had an idea he didn't *want* to understand.

He confounded himself by nodding instead.

SUPPER WAS a subdued affair. Madison kept rehearsing her words over and over in her mind. And she could tell that Brice was anxious and leery over her request to talk later.

The men ate without complaint—even though the spaghetti had too much salt and the slightly acrid taste of scorched meat. They helped themselves to extra servings of garlic bread while discussing the cattle and the range and the weather. Apparently someone named Harvey Langford had lost some of his herd to wolves. Randy volunteered to scout around.

Maddie abandoned any attempt to eat after only a few bites. She was so on edge, she could barely get anything past her throat. After giving Abbe a bottle, she stood. That apparently was a signal for the men. Chairs scraped and they all shot to their feet, practically tripping over themselves to get to the dishes—probably needing an excuse not to finish that awful meal.

Worried over what she intended to propose to Brice, Maddie excused herself and took Abbe into the nursery and laid her in the crib. She wound up the mobile and smiled as the plush animals twirled slowly, playing softly the tune of "Mary Had a Little Lamb."

Brice had done this for her.

But baby furniture and whimsical mobiles were small potatoes compared to what she was about to ask of him.

"It'll be okay, Abbe," she whispered, adjusting the soft pink blanket over her angelic miracle.

She left the door ajar and went into the living room. A fire crackled in the hearth.

Brice stood at the window—open again, she noticed. Oh, what must it have been like for him to be trapped in a well, a little boy alone, with no one to look for him.

Shadows from the flickering flames of the fire danced over the walls, over the solitary figure standing by the slightly open window. He looked so strong and capable with shoulders broad enough to carry the weight of the world.

Would they be broad enough to carry her request?

He turned, as though sensing her standing there.

"You wanted to talk?" he asked, a hint of wariness in his tone.

She didn't know how else to say it except flat-out.

"Yes. I was wondering...will you marry me?"

Chapter Seven

Brice went absolutely still. "Come again?"

"I know it sounds crazy, but hear me out."

"I'm listening."

"I've got to file Abbe's birth certificate, and I'm sure the Covingtons are searching every State data base in the country, looking for my name to show up. If I had a different name, if Abbe's name was different, they'd have less chance of finding us."

"You want to list me as the father of your baby? Give her my name?"

"Yes. Just your name. I won't ask anything else of you. In fact, I'll cook and keep house for you for free—for as long as you want."

He blinked, staring at her as though he were unable to formulate a coherent thought or word.

Her heart was pounding so hard she could barely hear past the roar in her ears. "I know I'm not doing my job right now. But I'll get better at it. I promise. We won't interfere in your life…much," she added. Of course they'd interrupt his life. And if she didn't get the hang of cooking, they'd all lose weight in the bargain—whether they wanted to or not.

"Say something," she pleaded when he just stood there like a statue. Well, who could blame him? It was a crazy idea.

She laced her hands together in front of her, trying to hide their trembling. He was going to turn her down. She knew it.

Shoulders slumping, she stared at the fire. "Never mind. It was a stupid request."

She heard him move then, and glanced over in time to see him grab his hat and coat and let himself out the front door.

Wonderful, Maddie chided herself. She'd handled that with all the finesse of a charging bull. She promised herself she wouldn't cry, yet felt the aching lump in her throat, anyway.

So much for heeding your lessons, she thought. She'd learned as a child not to make waves, to be agreeable, lest she be exchanged for a better kid, one who wouldn't rock the boat or demand too much.

Well, she'd certainly demanded plenty this time. And judging by the rigid set of Brice's jaw as he'd walked out of the house, Maddie figured it was time she packed her bags.

BRICE HAD CLEANED every piece of tack in the barn. Twice. There wasn't a speck of tarnish or rust on any of the silver. The smell of saddle soap and leather was heavy in the air. Every rope was coiled and hung symmetrically on the wall. Even his horse was giving him strange looks as he went to work on the stall, replacing perfectly good straw with a new layer.

He shouldn't be considering Madison's proposal, but he was.

He latched Samson's stall and moved to the open barn door. Stars winked in the inky sky, promising a clear but cold day tomorrow.

Cows lowed in the stock pens, and an owl hooted. All around him were the familiar sights and sounds he loved.

And that's what made him really consider Madison's crazy proposal. At one time he'd envisioned a dynasty of ranchers bearing his family's name.

But those images hadn't jelled. His brother, Kyle, had opted for corporate life instead of staying on the ranch. And if Kyle ever settled down, it wasn't likely that any of his future children would be interested in the Flying D legacy. A love of the land was bred by familiarity, by working every section, by living the life.

And as for children of his own, well, Sharon's accusation that it had been *his* fault they hadn't conceived had killed that dream.

So Madison's stunning, unexpected proposal took on a certain merit.

Still unsure of his answer, he walked slowly back to the house, automatically skirting the patch of ground where the well used to be. His father had filled it in shortly after the incident of his childhood, but superstition and caution had him giving it a wide berth regardless. He didn't trust the ground to hold him.

Just like he didn't trust most people not to let him down. Women at least.

He found her in his bedroom. He hardly recognized the room as his own, even though she hadn't moved anything. It held the essence of her presence, though, her springtime scent mingled with baby talc.

He noticed the open dresser drawers, saw the suitcase standing in the corner.

His heart lurched. She looked determined, yet so alone as she sat on the end of the bed.

"What are you doing?"

"I figured you'd want me to pack up."

He didn't know what he wanted. "You thought wrong."

She frowned at his churlish tone. "You walked out."

"I needed to think."

She nodded. "I understand. It was wrong of me to dump my prob—"

"I'll marry you."

Her head snapped up. "You will?"

"It makes a crazy sort of sense. I've got nothing to lose, provided you'll agree to sign a document waiving claim to my property."

"Of course. I wouldn't have it any other way." She picked at a loose thread on the quilt. "What made you decide to do it?"

He shrugged. "I care about what happens to you and Abbe. And I guess I like the idea of somebody out there having my name." He wouldn't tell her that family was his deepest yearning. That having a child—even if it was by default...and only for a little while—was an offer he couldn't turn down.

He'd had a hand in bringing that baby into this world—his world. It seemed fitting that she be the one he passed his legacy on to.

Now the hard part was going to be in keeping his emotional distance.

Regardless of the fact that he was helping Madison out, there was still the real possibility that she wouldn't stay.

And to that end, he needed to set a time limit, some parameters. If he was prepared, his heart couldn't suffer.

He was determined that wouldn't happen.

"We'll give it a three-month trial and reassess after that, get an annulment if you like. By that time you should know whether or not the grandparents have given up. And you'll have a real good idea of what winter on a remote cattle ranch is all about. It's a far cry from glamorized advertisements of dude ranches."

"Oh. I'm sure it'll be...fine." Maddie had expected a prenuptial agreement. If he hadn't suggested it, she would have. But she hadn't been prepared for talk of an annulment before they'd even said, "I do."

He nodded. "I'll call my attorney in the morning, have him fax over an agreement. If you're up to it, we'll go into church this Sunday. After the services, I'm sure Pastor Glen won't mind performing a quick ceremony."

"I'll be up to it. Thank you."

She watched him walk out of the room, saw him automatically duck his head in the doorway, even though he wasn't wearing his hat. The habit of a tall man.

A really wonderful man.

Goodness! Her heart was racing and her palms were damp.

He'd actually agreed to marry her! It was what she wanted, so why was she suddenly feeling so bereft? As though there was a detail missing.

Like a handshake to seal the bargain. Or a kiss...

Oh, Madison, don't be greedy.

HER WEDDING DAY dawned bright and crisp. Ice dripped from the eaves as the sun attempted to pierce the freezing temperatures.

Brice had been up before daylight, tending to the animals or whatever else he did at those ungodly hours.

But Maddie was struggling with another problem.

What to wear to church services—and to her wedding.

Her selection of clothes was minimal. And not a single thing remotely resembled bridal.

Brice passed by her open bedroom door, then doubled back and paused in the doorway. "Better shake a leg, sunshine. It'll take about forty-five minutes to get to the church. Services start at ten."

She tightened the sash of her robe, still peering into the closet. Articles of clothing were strewn on the bed behind her. What should have been the happiest day in her life was starting off in disgust.

Then again, this wasn't a real marriage in the fairy-tale sense. It was silly to have giddy expectations under the circumstances.

"Problem?" he asked.

"Half my clothes still don't fit. And what does fit doesn't seem suitable for church." *Or my wedding.*

He came up behind her, smelling of crisp, wintery air and hay. "You should have said something. We could've placed an overnight order through one of the catalogues."

Just that quickly, her mood lightened. She glanced at him,

feeling an unexpected thrill at the way his hat was cocked low over his brow, the way his height and breadth surrounded her in a protective cocoon.

"I'm already on a first-name basis with the UPS guy. Many more trips out here and people are gonna talk."

"They've been talking for years. I do a lot of mail-ordering."

"How did you get on so many catalogue lists?" Especially Victoria's Secret.

"My ex spent a lot of time and money ordering stuff. When she left, she got a cash settlement. I got the bills and the junk mail."

"You could have had them stopped."

He shrugged. "It's convenient."

It felt strange discussing his ex-wife on their wedding day. Again, Madison had to remind herself that this wasn't the everyday, run-of-the-mill marriage.

And she had to keep reminding herself not to wish it were.

"How about that green dress you were wearing the other night?"

Thermal cotton instead of silk. She shook her head. "It has baby spit-up on the shoulder."

He flicked through the sparse hangers in the closet, pulled out a wool skirt and soft blue tunic sweater. "This would look pretty with your eyes."

Astonished, she looked at him, and couldn't find her voice. He was so close. It was their wedding day. They were standing in his bedroom, and she wasn't wearing a stitch under her robe.

Possibilities flitted through her mind. She saw his pupils widen, whether it was from desire or the shading of his hat she wasn't sure.

The moment spun out, charged.

Then he stepped back. "We're going to be late."

Maddie let out a trembling breath, watched the shift of his

broad shoulders beneath his chambray shirt as he left the room, watched his hat brush the top of the doorjamb.

Get a grip, she told herself. Just because it was her wedding day didn't mean she should start thinking about sexy things like her wedding *night.*

But there was something really special about Brice DeWitt. He was good at protecting, she realized, the type of man who quietly took care of everyone around him. He employed more ranch hands than he needed, hired any old drifter who showed up, agreed to marry a woman he barely knew.

She wondered who took care of him, and vowed that from this day on, for as long as she was with him, she would make it her job to give back to him, to do for him in any way she could think of.

She couldn't get the skirt zipped all the way up, but the tunic sweater hid the fact. A pair of tights and knee-high boots completed her wedding ensemble.

With Abbe strapped in her car seat they pulled up at the small, white Methodist church. In the back seat, Moe looked clearly relieved that they'd finally arrived. He'd insisted Madison sit in the front with Brice, and had winced over every bump in the road that had jostled the baby.

Brice shut off the Jeep's engine. "Stay put," he said to Maddie, then came around to the passenger door and opened it for her, giving her a hand out. "You want to hold Abbe, or carry her in the baby seat?"

"Since she's sleeping for the moment, let's leave her in the seat. If she fusses we'll go to plan B."

"She wouldn't dare fuss in church."

"Ha. Optimist."

Brice ended up carrying the infant seat, since Maddie wasn't too sure about her footing on the ice. The four of them entered the church, causing a stir of both speculation and welcome.

Women cooed over the baby, Brice kept a fairly stoic expression on his face, and Moe beamed like a proud grandpa—from a safe distance of course.

Maddie felt out of place and conspicuous. These were Brice's friends and neighbors. What would they think when they found out he was marrying her?

It wasn't as though they could admit to their reasons. The less people knew, the safer it was for Maddie and Abbe.

Seated in the back pew—so they could make a quick exit if Abbe threw a fit—Maddie voiced her uneasiness. She leaned close to Brice's ear. "What are we going to tell people about our sudden marriage?"

He turned slowly, glanced down at her. "That Abbe's my daughter, and I'm finally making an honest woman out of you."

Her heart pounded like a drum at the sensual drawl in his voice, the lazy tip of his head, the utter intimacy of his look. She cleared her throat. "But Doc knows that I'm just the house-keeper."

The corners of his lips pulled into a sexy grin. "So, he'll think it was love at first sight. Especially if the men mention your cooking."

She narrowed her eyes. "Those are fighting words, DeWitt. And I'm betting you'll eat them before long." She'd left herself wide-open with that statement, but he didn't comment as she'd thought he would.

Sitting next to him, their thighs and shoulders brushing, was having a profound effect on her equilibrium. Especially when he graced her with that sexy grin. His aftershave teased her senses, smelling clean and masculine and making her heart race. She'd forgotten how sensual the scent of a man's cologne could be.

Moe leaned over the baby—who was between them on the pew. "There's plenty of time for jawin', but the good Lord's house ain't one of them. And it ain't rightly none of my business, but if the two of you keep givin' the other those cow eyes, there'll be talk from here to Montana."

Brice leaned forward, resting his arm on Maddie's lap, so he could speak to his friend. She held her breath, trying *not* to respond to the warmth of that innocent contact.

"There'll be plenty to talk about, anyway, after the wedding today."

"The what!" Moe's shout rang like a cowbell in the church.

Everyone stopped and stared. Maddie slid lower in her seat. Moe's ears turned bright red, and he gave apologetic nods to several parishioners. Brice calmly leaned back in his seat, this time speaking softly over her head.

"Madison and I are getting married after church services. I'd be happy if you'd stand as my best man."

"Ya might'a given me a little more warning about this shindig," Moe whispered. "And 'course I'll be standin' up fer ya." He gave a jerky nod, rocked the infant seat a couple of times to make sure his outburst hadn't disturbed the baby, then reached over and patted Maddie on the shoulder. "Well, that's just fine. Yep, that'll be real fine."

A group of women sat down in front of them, a young brunette in a fancy Western skirt and embroidered blouse pausing to bestow a beaming smile on Brice. She barely glanced at Maddie and gave a small frown in the baby's direction.

Madison bristled.

Evidently, Moe did, too.

"This ain't no dance social, Miss Adeline, and it's pure sacrilege to be flirtin' in the church house. B'sides, the boy's off the market. It's his weddin' day."

Adeline's dark, perfectly arched brows shot up, and her expression fell. This time she did look at Maddie, and Maddie stared right back, thankful she was wearing her contact lenses and not the thick glasses. It gave her a small measure of confidence—never mind that her skirt wasn't zipped all the way. Clearly, Adeline's waistline was less than twenty-four inches. Maddie despised the woman on that point alone.

"You're getting married, Brice?" Her voice carried.

Madison nearly groaned. They'd agreed to a quiet affair after everyone was gone.

There weren't more than twenty people in the church, but every head, it seemed, turned in their direction.

Brice casually slipped an arm across Madison's shoulders.

"As a matter of fact, we are."

The pastor was about to call for a hymn and begin his welcome, but chaos ensued. People left their seats, determined to congratulate, to plan, to express opinions and ask questions.

Introductions and handshakes and hugs were passed out like a long-awaited gathering at a family reunion. No one judged or looked askance—except for Adeline. They accepted both Maddie and the wedding news with enthusiasm and welcome.

Maddie was unsure what to say or how to act. She'd never been part of a community before, never had a family to call her own.

Not that she actually had one now.

"Well," Pastor Glen said, chuckling. "We're not at the greeting-your-neighbor part, but a little variety in the routine is good."

Madison noticed the pastor sharing a look with Brice, noticed Brice's slight nod.

Her eyes widened. She got a bad feeling. "What was that about?" she whispered, her voice hissing.

The preacher answered her question.

"We've got a special event going on this morning. Most of you seem to have caught wind of the DeWitt wedding. I'm thinking since you all are completely out of order and in a festive mood, we'll just have the ceremony now instead of the sermon. There's nothing more uplifting than joining two people together in the house of God."

Oh, Lord. Now she felt really guilty.

Lying in church for the sake of expediency—or safety.

Promising to love, honor and cherish until death do they

part—especially in light of the fact that they'd already discussed an annulment in three months' time.

Then another thought careened out of nowhere.

Didn't an annulment mean an unconsummated union?

For three months she would have to look at this man, live with him, and not have sex?

Oh, Madison, stop it. You're in church, for crying out loud. That line of thinking was surely inappropriate.

The crowd moved along to take their seats. Several of the ladies offered to mind the baby, which sparked a brief tussle with Moe until it was pointed out that he'd be needed to stand up for Brice.

Nancy Adams finally won the honor of holding the baby.

"Careful with the neck if you go takin' her out of the seat," Moe lectured.

Nancy laughed. "I'm a nurse, Moe Bertelli. I think I can manage."

"Humph," was all he said and herded Maddie and Brice out of the pew.

It was the weirdest ceremony Maddie had ever seen. As she made her way up the aisle at Brice's side, additional introductions to her neighbors were being made.

Strange to get married and not even know who was on the guest list.

But she knew Brice, or felt like she'd known him all her life. Looking at him made her knees go weak.

"You okay with this, sunshine? You can back out if you want."

"No. I'm fine." Or would be if he'd stop looking at her that way. He wore a saddle-suede blazer and dark brown pants with a piped, chocolate-colored Western shirt. The silver slide on his braided leather bolo tie matched the silver buckle on his belt.

Knowing she shouldn't be looking at his belt—especially in church—she lowered her eyes even farther. Ostrich-skin boots the color of cognac were polished to a sheen, and she imagined the bottoms of those expensive puppies had never seen the soil of a cow pen.

He passed his dark brown hat to Moe for safekeeping.

"Flowers," Letty Springer said, popping out of her seat. "We can't have a bride without flowers." She plucked an arrangement of silk roses out of a vase by the altar, snatched a light blue ribbon right out of her daughter's hair and tied a perfect bow in a matter of seconds.

Maddie was impressed.

Letty wasn't happy with the results, though. "I'd thought to get 'borrowed and blue' all in one whack, but it hardly shows up."

Brice reached in his coat pocket and pulled out a blue silk bandanna. "Try this."

"Oh, perfect," Letty said. She tied the bandanna into a fluffy bow around the stems of the silk roses. "There you go, darlin'. It picks up the color in your sweater very nicely. And a girl shouldn't be so rushed and put on the spot on her wedding day. This will make it feel more festive."

Maddie was touched. "Thank you, Letty."

"Don't even mention it. Since your Mama's not here to see to the little details, I'm honored to do my part."

Maddie nearly lost her battle with her emotions then. She'd never let herself dream about a fairy-tale wedding with all the trimmings, much less having a mother there to fuss.

This spur-of-the-moment affair, in this little community church with its friendly people was ten times better than the fairy tale.

She looked at the impromptu bouquet in her hands, thinking it was the most beautiful thing she'd ever seen. Brice's silk bandanna brushed her fingers, giving her a semblance of calm.

Brice touched her cheek, searching her eyes. Her gaze clung to his. He made her want, made her forget all about her fears and worries. He made her feel safe.

And he made her yearn for this to be a *real* marriage.

"Ready?" he asked softly.

"More than ready." She saw his brows lift, saw the amusement in his deep blue eyes. Heat burned her cheeks, and her palms went damp around the soft plastic stems of the roses.

Pastor Glen gave a joyous laugh that invited participation. "Looks like we'd better get this ceremony moving along."

Maddie ducked her head, determined to conduct herself with a little more decorum. She was looking at Brice like a starving cougar at a cattlemen's feast. And he was looking back in much the same way. At least it appeared that way. Added to that the fact there was a baby present, before nuptials had even been completed, she felt more like a sinner in church than a bride.

"Is there someone to give you away, Miss Carlyle?" the preacher asked.

Maddie opened her mouth to say no, thinking that she'd been given away years ago by a father who'd never even looked back and a mother who could care less.

Moe shuffled his feet. "I reckon that'd be me—if it ain't against the rules to do double duty, bein' the best man and all. And if it's okay with you, Miss Maddie."

She nodded, and there really were tears this time, tears that Brice noticed and gently brushed away with a callused thumb.

"All right, then," the pastor said. "If the bride and groom would join hands and face each other, we'll proceed in joining you together in holy matrimony."

There were sighs from the people in the church, a sniff or two as ladies dabbed at tears, and Abbe even got her two cents' worth in by letting out a burp that echoed within the church walls and sent the congregation into chuckles.

But Maddie hardly knew what was being said, what she was saying in return. It was all a blur. There was only Brice: his strong hands holding hers, his gaze steady and intense and so unreadable.

When the preacher prompted him, he produced a ring and slipped it on her finger. She was stunned.

Staring at the braided circle of silver which was a perfect

fit and signified unbroken eternity, Maddie completely missed her cue to say "I do."

It was the sudden silence in the church and Brice's slight squeeze of her hand that alerted her to the oversight.

"Miss Carlyle?" Pastor Glen prompted.

"Oh, yes. I do." The words were filled with more meaning than was warranted for this particular ceremony.

And it was at that moment that Maddie realized something very important and earthshaking.

She really meant the words.

She was in love with Brice DeWitt.

In love with his gentleness, his ethics, his heart that he guarded so carefully—in love with the man as a whole.

Lord above, what a mess. That wasn't part of the bargain.

"By the powers vested in me by God and the State of Wyoming, I now pronounce you man and wife. Brice, you may kiss your bride."

This was the part that was going to be tricky, Brice thought. She was looking at him with wide, cornflower blue eyes filled with emotions he couldn't define. When he placed a hand at the small of her back and urged her closer, he nearly groaned. Her heat scorched him. Her lips, when he bent his head to seal the bargain, were soft and warm and welcoming, if a little timid.

And all the while, their eyes remained open, locked in a silent communication of want and need and wariness.

For the space of several heartbeats, his mind went blank of every thought. All he could do was feel—and want even more.

And he felt a little like a hypocrite.

They were simply sealing a bargain, a formal extension of the prenuptial paper she'd signed last night. She hadn't even hesitated when he'd presented the faxed document to her. There was no reason why that immediate compliance should have given him such a punch in the heart. It was what he'd wanted, what he'd requested.

This wasn't a real marriage.

And that, basically, was the problem. Everything in his life seemed to be temporary—the cows were temporary until they were sold at the market, the ranch hands were temporary until they moved on to the next spread, his dad had been temporary until death, his mother and ex-wife only biding time until they could stand it no longer and left.

How long would it be before Madison left? And could he keep his heart intact until then?

He'd have to. Everything in his life came and went like nodding acquaintances met on the road. Everything except the land. That's the only attachment he could allow himself. He wouldn't allow Madison and Abbe to take a piece of him when they left. Because he would never recover.

He felt her hand slide up his jacket, rest over his heart, and he wanted to go on kissing her for a lifetime.

He stepped back instead.

The congregation clapped, not realizing the turmoil that swirled in his gut as he stared down at his new wife.

His temporary wife.

Chapter Eight

The day had been a long one, with the church folks insisting on turning the usual Sunday potluck into a reception in celebration of the wedding. Then Letty Springer had opened the store so Madison could get a supply of baby formula and toiletries.

By the time they got home, Madison was looking worn and frazzled and Brice was more high-strung than a wild bronc at a rodeo.

The details of a wedding night hadn't been part of their sealed bargain, but he was sure thinking about them.

And if he'd stayed in the house one more second, smelled the delicate scent of her perfume, felt the brush of her soft breasts as she reached past him to prepare Abbe's bottle, he very likely would have done something he'd sorely regret.

So he ended up in the bunkhouse on his wedding night, playing a game of poker with the men—who were giving both him and his black mood a wide berth.

From the open window came the relentless sound of Abbe's cries.

"Young'un's been at it for a while now," Moe commented.

Brice didn't answer. He had a pair of deuces in his hand and nothing to go with it. He tossed down three cards and Moe dealt him the appropriate number in return.

"Heard tell some babies get a bellyache when you take 'em out in the wind," Dan commented, upping the ante in the pot.

"Humph," Moe muttered. "It was all them ladies passin' the little bit around like she was a baby doll."

Brice still didn't comment.

Abbe's pitiful cries continued, carried along by the wind. He picked up his cards. Two ladies and another deuce.

Full house.

Yeah, he certainly had that. A wife and baby and full house.

And that baby was sounding like she was dying of a broken heart. And what about Madison? When he'd left her, she'd looked worn to a frazzle.

"Call," Randy said, the only one of the foursome who wasn't looking toward the house and pretending that he wasn't.

Brice tossed his cards on the table. "I'm out." Never mind that there was fifty bucks in the pot and he could have won hands down.

Randy whooped over winning with a measly pair of sixes.

Moe shot the younger man a scowl.

"What?" Randy asked, clearly bewildered. "My sixes beat anything the rest of you've got."

"Cain't you hear that little baby cryin'? You know, for a feller who could track a gnat in a blizzard, you sure can be dense," Moe said.

Brice scraped back his chair and stood. "I'd better go check on them."

"Probably should," Moe said with a relieved look. "'Spect I'll just walk on over and keep ya company. I got a hankerin' for a cup of chocolate."

Dan rose, fell into step. "Come to think of it, chocolate sounds good to me, too."

Randy, stuffing money into his pockets, grabbed his hat and followed, clearly surprised that everyone was deserting him.

Brice told himself it was the cold air that made his ground-eating steps brisk. It wasn't because he was worried about Madison and the baby.

His family.

Something fluttered in his stomach, and it felt like hope. He dismissed it.

When he opened the back door, the decibel level of noise was earsplitting. How could something that little make so much racket?

Madison was sweating, and the kitchen window, normally ajar, was pushed wide-open. No wonder they'd been able to hear the cries so easily.

She glanced up, and he could have sworn he saw tears in her eyes. He moved to her, gazed down at the unhappy baby in her arms, touched the backs of his fingers to Madison's cheek. Was it just that his hands were cold or was she running a fever?

"You look like you could use a break."

"I don't know what's wrong with her. Do you think I should call the doctor?"

If he wasn't mistaken, Madison needed a doctor more than the baby did. "Let me take a turn with her first."

He lifted the baby from her arms, feeling the usual softening when he held her, though he still felt awkward, as though his big hands would crush the little thing.

"Here, now, princess. What's all the fuss?"

At the sound of his voice, Abbe's wail tapered to a snuffle. He felt proud and smug.

Madison obviously didn't appreciate his smugness.

"Now why wouldn't she do that for me?"

He searched her features, saw the utter weariness in her eyes, the flags of color on her cheeks. "You're running a fever, aren't you."

She shrugged. "Probably from the tail end of this infection."

"Why don't you go on to bed. Between the four of us," he indicated Moe, Dan and Randy with a nod, "we can hold down the fort with the baby."

"I'm not so sure. She's in a mood."

"Boss's right, Miss Maddie," Moe said. "You jest get yourself some rest. I done a good job of holding the young'un before. You can trust us not to let the neck flop or nothing."

At the mention of necks, Brice checked to make sure he had it supported properly.

"She probably needs changing," Maddie hedged. The four men hovered, looking out of place and scared to death—though they were making a brave show otherwise.

She found it interesting how these cowboys were all bluff. They portrayed rough, tough guys, yet every head turned when the baby was around, and it was so obvious that softer emotions emerged—even though they made comical efforts to hide them.

And Brice was the most interesting of all. He tried so hard to appear detached, yet she'd seen the way he touched Abbe, the way he looked at her with such profound yearning. More than once she'd caught him making goofy faces at the baby when nobody was looking.

He guarded his heart so closely. Yet it was clear that he needed to open it.

And it was clear that she was exhausted and wouldn't be any good to anyone if she didn't get some rest. She felt bad for shirking her responsibilities—again—but was too grateful for the offer to toss it back.

"We'll take care of her," Brice said. "You go rest."

"Okay. Just for a while."

Brice wanted to pick her up and carry her to bed, to tuck her in and make sure she took care of herself properly. The woman had been through so many trials in the past couple of weeks, it was no wonder she was at the end of her rope.

But tucking her in wasn't an option right now. Aside from the fact that it would test his tenuous control, he had the baby to look after.

And three crusty ranch hands hovering like concerned mother hens.

And the baby blanket was definitely wet.

"We can do this," he said to his men once Madison had left. "We'll need a diaper, clothes and a dry blanket."

The guys scrambled to round up the necessary items.

"I got the clothes," Randy said proudly, holding up a pink undershirt he'd grabbed from a folded stack of laundry on top of the washing machine. He measured the outfit against the size of his hand. "Awful dang small if you ask me."

Moe snatched the tiny cotton outfit out of his hands. "Nobody asked ya. Swear, Toval, you're 'bout worthless as teats on a bull."

"What's wrong with that shirt?" Randy griped when Moe tossed it back and picked out a footed, one-piece sleeper.

"It's the dead of winter. How'd you like to sleep in yer undershirt when there was perfectly good long johns sittin' right under your nose?"

"I don't sleep in long johns."

"If you ladies are done arguing fashion advice, I could do with a little more speed," Brice said, wondering which was the best way to go about changing the infant. She'd stopped crying now, probably out of sheer fear over what her bungling babysitters would do next.

Dan spread blankets on the kitchen table, and Brice carefully laid Abbe down in the center of them.

"Watch the neck!" Moe hollered.

"If you say that one more time, I'm going to get my gun."

"Yer not exactly an expert, ya know."

"And you are?" Now Brice was starting to sweat. The baby's legs were like spindly twigs. Pulling them out of the pajamas scared him spitless.

"Least I got more years on you. Ought to qualify me for havin' more knowledge."

"Well, use your knowledge and hold the baby's foot."

It was an utter fiasco. Four grown men—experts at roping and herding wily animals—trying in vain to pin down one tiny baby long enough to accomplish a diaper change.

Brice's hands alone were bigger than Abbe's whole body. Add three more sets and it was causing more problems than help.

"I don't think you've got that diaper folded right," Randy volunteered.

"That's the least of my worries," Brice countered.

"My sister used disposable diapers," Dan said. "Personally, it'd make me feel a lot better if we had something with tapes on it rather than using that safety pin."

Sweat was running down Brice's temples now. Abbe was scrunching up her face to voice her disapproval with their ineptness.

"Somebody open the window. Shuller, since you're such a font of information, why don't you put your fingers in here so I won't stick her."

"The window is open," Moe answered for Dan. "And use your own finger and stop your bellyaching. We could'a roped and branded fifty calves in the time it's takin' you to truss up one little baby. Danged if you ain't a sorry excuse for a new papa."

The reminder that as of today this baby was a DeWitt did two things to Brice. It made his stomach flutter like a migration of spring butterflies—and it made him determined.

Where before he'd been bumbling around like a tiptoeing Brahma bull at a tea party, a certain masculine pride steadied his hands.

The diaper pin drew blood—his, thank God—but he got it secured, managed to snap on a pair of ruffled waterproof pants over it, then wrestled Abbe's twiglike arms and legs into the pajamas.

Okay. Not his best work, but it would do. "Somebody grab a bottle."

Randy opened the refrigerator. "Breast milk or formula."

Moe scowled. "That's a dang fool question to ask."

"Isn't either. There's two here. And that's how they're labeled."

"Formula," Brice said before a dispute could form. Besides, this being his wedding night and all, he didn't want any reminders about breasts, or women, or where babies get their milk. Never mind that it was just a note on a bottle.

The next fiasco was over whether or not to pour the milk in a pan or heat the bottle in water.

Brice left the men to duke it out. Other than a few snuffles now and again, Abbe's eyes were closed, her little body relaxing like a tiny feather in his arms. He cradled her close, swaying slightly, feeling his heart swell and his throat ache.

Abigail DeWitt. She might not have come from his seed, but pride swelled to overflowing. He had an urge to take her outside, to show her the stock and the buildings and the land, to tell her all about what would one day be hers....

Her legacy as the only DeWitt to carry on his name when he was gone. He wondered if he could talk her into keeping his name when she one day married.

Okay, he was getting ahead of himself here.

How could a guy keep his emotional distance from something so perfect as this little infant? A baby who now bore his family's name.

"Well, lookie there," Moe whispered. "She done fell asleep."

"Yeah," Brice said, equally as quietly. "Thanks for the help, guys. I can take it from here."

Moe herded the other men out the door and followed.

Brice shut off the light, leaving only the soft glow of the lamp over the stove. Carefully supporting the baby with one arm, he reached up and eased the window almost shut.

"I don't imagine we could hire ourselves out as competent baby-sitters," he said softly to the sleeping child, "but we muddled through. Let's go check on your mama."

The quiet in the house reminded him how tired he was.

He'd put in a full day's work and gotten married to boot.

Not your everyday occurrence on the Flying D.

Madison was curled on her side, sleeping soundly. He stood

there a moment, just looking at her. The lamp burned by the side of the bed, casting an amber glow over her blond hair.

What would it be like if these two ladies who'd literally dropped into his life were *really* his?

He shook his head. That kind of thinking could get him in trouble. And he wouldn't be obsessing over such things if he weren't so tired, he told himself.

Spying the dresser drawer he'd rigged as a bassinet, he laid the sleeping baby down. Right now, the nursery seemed too far away. As tired as he was, and as heavily as Madison was sleeping, there was every possibility that neither one of them would wake if the baby cried.

Sitting carefully on the side of the bed so he wouldn't disturb Madison, he watched the baby sleep, making sure she was actually going to stay that way for a while.

Man alive, how could something so small wear out a houseful of adults this way?

Madison shifted, and he whipped around. She was still asleep, had kicked the covers off. Her cotton gown had ridden up. Hand hovering in indecision, he finally pulled it down, then tucked the blankets back around her.

Softly, with the backs of his fingers, he tested the heat in her cheeks. Warm, but not hot. They probably wouldn't need to call the doctor.

Shoulders aching, he tugged off his damp shirt and eased down beside her on the bed, telling himself he'd just lie here for a few minutes, just to make sure she or Abbe didn't need him.

THE SOUND of Abbe's cries pierced Maddie's subconscious. She felt warmth and had an urge to snuggle closer. Her foot connected with a hairy thigh.

Her eyes popped open the rest of the way. "Oh!"

"Mumph," Brice muttered and threw an arm over his eyes. "S'okay. I'll get her." Half-asleep, he rolled over and nearly fell out of the bed.

Maddie made a grab for the sheet, then snatched her glasses off the nightstand. From the soft glow of the bedside lamp, she read the illuminated dial of the clock—5:00 a.m.

"What are you doing?"

He halted mid-stride, blinked his eyes like a barn owl in a stupor and stared at her as though he'd never seen her in his life.

She pulled the quilt higher. Ridiculous. He'd already seen more of her than any man had a right to, but still, she felt nervous.

The man was practically naked. Well, shirtless, anyway, and the sight of all that masculine chest had her entertaining all sorts of fantasies.

"I'm getting the baby." Yawning, he raked his fingers through his hair.

"I meant, what were you doing in my bed?"

His brow rose. "Though I'm not worth a damn before my coffee, I think it's called sleeping. And technically, it's *my* bed." He picked up the baby. "Well no wonder you're raising the rooftop, Abbe. You're soaked clear through. I could have sworn I corrected that last night."

Despite the jolt and sleepy confusion of finding herself in bed with him, Maddie smiled, her heart melting at the sight of this rugged, virile man talking softly to her baby.

When he moved back to the side of the bed, she held out her arms and accepted the wiggling baby. Abbe stopped crying and opened round eyes, staring up at her mother.

"You decided yet if I should be shot at dawn?"

She glanced up at him and grinned sheepishly. "Sorry. Here you pull baby-sitting duty, and I end up acting ungrateful as all get-out. You caught me by surprise is all."

He touched the backs of his fingers to her cheek. "Looks like a decent night's sleep did you good."

"Mmm, and Abbe seems much more agreeable when I'm not climbing the walls." She looked at him, a little sorry that he hadn't taken off his jeans along with his shirt. After the initial shock of seeing him half-undressed, she was hungry to see more. "Thank you for taking over last night."

He shrugged and grabbed his T-shirt, pulling it over his head. His chest muscles flexed and rippled. Maddie sucked in a breath and nearly choked.

Pulling the body-hugging cotton over his washboard stomach, he tucked it into the waistband of his jeans. "You probably would have split a gut laughing at the sight we made. No telling if her diaper's even still on."

Oh, she loved the way his face softened into boyish charm when he smiled that way.

Her husband, she thought, feeling a giddy thrill shoot through her. Never mind that he only claimed that title on paper, she didn't see the harm in giving the fantasy a little nudge. It was her secret.

"You obviously did something right. Did she sleep through the night, or was I just too tired to hear her?"

"She fussed around two o'clock, but I put that sucky thing in her mouth, and she settled back down."

"Thank goodness for the invention of pacifiers." The diaper was around the baby's knees. Maddie smiled, quickly stripped off the sodden clothes and accepted the change of clothes Brice held out to her. She really was feeling better today.

Their fingers touched, and his thigh brushed her hip as he stood close, watching over her shoulder as she changed the baby.

She paused, looked at him, found him watching her instead of the task she was managing to accomplish with a great deal of efficiency. Oh, this felt right. Waking up together, sharing the responsibility of the baby.

It made it hard not to imagine that this was a real marriage. Abbe kicked her feet, reminding Maddie of her duties.

"Baby monitors," Brice said suddenly.

"Excuse me?" She shoved her slipping glasses back in place, looked up at him.

"I saw them in the catalogue."

Oh, Lord, the UPS man would be out again soon. "DeWitt, you are a maniac with mail-order and credit cards. You've got to stop buying stuff for us."

"It's for me."

She frowned so she wouldn't smile. The man was by far too sexy. And too generous. "How so?"

"So we can hear the baby when she cries from the nursery. It'll save steps. That way we can tell if it's just a fidgeting cry or one that means business."

For several beats, her heart went absolutely still, then started up again with a pounding vengeance. He kept saying "we," as though they were a real family. She told herself it was a figure of speech, a slip of the tongue. It didn't mean anything, and she was being foolish, trying to assign a deeper motive.

"And you think you can tell the difference? So far, I've only been able to identify one kind of cry. The flat-out, no-holds-barred, I-haven't-the-slightest-idea-what-it-means kind."

"You're operating under a handicap. As soon as you get stronger, you'll gain those instincts."

She was feeling stronger and stronger by the minute, if the butterflies in her stomach were any indication. As for instincts, a few were screaming loud and clear right now.

The instincts that told her controlling her growing desire for this wonderful, thoughtful cowboy were going to be nigh unto impossible.

"WHAT THE HELL happened to my jeans?"

Brice's roar nearly made Maddie jump out of her chair. Her head snapped up, her fingers poised over the keys of the computer.

"I did the laundry and hemmed them for you." Considering the fact that she was no domestic goddess, she felt fairly proud of herself for that little chore. She glanced around the desk so she could get a good look at his feet, pleased with the length. Pretty darn good for just guessing, she thought smugly.

"Why would you do something like that?"

An all-too-familiar bad feeling edged in, fraying her nerves. Her smile dimmed.

"I thought I was doing you a favor. I mean, you being a bachelor and all...I figured there weren't any tailors close by. Your pants were so long, they bunched on the tops of your boots."

"They're *supposed* to fit that way. Now I look like I'm expecting a flood or competing for sissy of the year award."

She stared at him for a full ten seconds, all six foot five inches of virile, handsome-as-sin cowboy. He couldn't look like a sissy if he tried.

Sidetracked, replaying the last few lines of their conversation in her mind, she realized he hadn't contradicted her calling him a bachelor. An unexpected pang stung her insides, and she chided the foolishness. Their marriage was barely a week old. Of course he'd forget.

And she had to stop forgetting it wasn't a *real* marriage. Only a kind act from a very special man.

A man who at the moment was looking really appalled and trying his best to pretend otherwise.

"You wear them that way on purpose? What? As a fashion statement?"

"It has nothing to do with fashion. I don't care to have the hem of my pants riding clear up to my shins where snow or debris can slip down the boot tops. Besides, it looks dorky."

"Oh." Embarrassment turned her palms sweaty. She'd screwed up again. Her citified roots were showing. The only cowboys she'd been around were the urban type, who wore flashy colors and spit-shined boots.

And Brice's working boots obviously hadn't seen a polish cloth since they'd come off the factory assembly line.

"I'm sorry. I was only trying to help." She'd had to cut the material, so there was no way she could offer to lengthen them a bit. Darn it, she'd thought she'd done something right at last—especially with the mess she was still making of the cooking.

So much for making it her job to take care of him. He'd be lucky to even survive her!

Brice sighed and ordered himself to calm down. Her soft blue eyes held hurt and embarrassment. And he'd put it there.

"They're not that bad." He pinched the material and gave it a tug. It didn't help.

She perked up. "They're not?"

He shook his head, unable to compound the lie. "Did you, uh, do any of the others?"

Her gazed lowered, and she suddenly became highly interested in the numbers on the ledger she'd been working on.

"Madison?"

"A couple."

He could barely hear her. "A couple?"

"Three." She pulled her lips between her teeth, hiding a smile, her fingers drumming on the desk. "Will the guys really call you a sissy?"

The little imp. Despite the fiasco with his jeans, she flat-out charmed him. In some areas she was so confident, and in others she didn't seem to have the sense God gave a stray dogie. But her heart was in the right place. He vowed to quietly—and quickly—place a catalogue order for more jeans.

He cleared his throat, dragging his gaze away from the utter enticement of her full lips. "They wouldn't dare."

She let out a self-deprecating laugh. "I swear I've never been so inept in my life. I've managed to live almost twenty-nine years without starving myself—never mind that my awful cooking should suggest otherwise."

"It's not that bad," he felt compelled to say. *Almost twenty-nine years.* She had a birthday coming up really soon.

Her laughter trilled again. "It might not be, if I could remember to put baking *powder* instead of soda in the biscuits."

"Easy mistake. They look pretty much the same." Before he got himself in any deeper, he focused on the papers spread before her. "Making any headway with all that stuff?"

"Oh, absolutely. Here is where I excel, making sense out of invoices and receipts. A few keystrokes, and chaos becomes order. Of course, you might not agree since you view computers as monsters."

"I never said they were monsters. Just that I didn't know how to use them." She'd been true to her word and kept everything separate, so when he came into his office late at night to catch up on paperwork, he'd been able to find exactly what he needed. Much to his surprise, though, she'd dealt with quite a few of his things in his "to do" pile.

"I have a laptop that I brought with me, and some killer software."

"Whoa, there, sunshine. Now you're talking way over my head."

She waved an airy hand, making him want to grab those busy, delicate fingers and hold on.

"Never mind. When you have the time, I'll give you a crash course in the lingo and workings of the thing. But as I said, this is my area of expertise. If you like, I can file your income taxes for you."

"I usually wait until the last possible minute. It's only the middle of January now." And by the time the IRS deadline rolled around, their three months would be up. If she even lasted that long. It was foolish to make plans beyond each day.

"We don't have to mail them. But I can get a head start." She chewed the end of her pencil, drummed her fingers some more. "I really am a top-notch accountant. I'd have to check the regulations on allowable deductions for cattle ranchers..." Her words trailed off and she shrugged. "But if you'd rather have your own CPA handle it, I'll understand."

She looked vulnerable all of a sudden, as though expecting rejection. Her chin tipped forward, giving the impression she was braced for whatever he threw at her, as though she'd had to fight for everything she got in life.

She had the smoothest, clearest skin he'd ever seen on a woman, the type of skin that invited a man to touch, to enjoy. No caked-on makeup like Sharon had been fond of wearing.

Behind the lenses of her glasses, her lashes were dark and lush in contrast to her pale yellow hair.

He glanced away, unable to keep looking for fear that he would touch.

And if he touched, it would be all over. Because he wouldn't stop there.

He stood. "If you want to tackle the taxes, have at it. Just don't overdo."

"I won't. And I want to do this for you, Brice. You've done so much for Abbe and me, and I want to return the favor."

"You don't owe me anything."

She raised a brow. "Think about it. You've been my doctor, my employer, my baby-sitter, my personal shopper and my husband. And in return, I've ripped your sheets, burned your dinners, fallen asleep on you and taken over your bed, and—" She stopped, ducked her head. "Well, anyway, you get the picture. According to my calculations, my account's really far in the red."

He wished she hadn't mentioned that part about the bed. Reminding him that he was her husband was jolting enough. Mentioning husband and bed in practically the same sentence was hell on his all-too-vivid imagination and his very active libido.

He backed up a step, really needing to get out of this room. "I'm not keeping score." He turned, made it to the door, then paused. "Uh, Madison?"

"Yes?"

"The next time you come within nodding acquaintance with a needle and thread, do me a favor and resist, would you?"

He glanced back in time to see her sheepish smile blossom. She nodded, and his heart nearly drummed out of his chest.

Hell, if he was smart, he'd go out and throw himself into the ice-coated horse trough.

Chapter Nine

With the cookbook open on the counter and an apron tied around her waist, Maddie studiously ignored the mess in the kitchen. She'd been here almost a month and she still kept forgetting to adopt the clean-as-you-go method.

"I'm going to cook a decent meal if it kills me," she said to Abbe, who happily kicked her stocking feet against the infant seat. "You doubt me, munchkin? Wait and see. We're handicapped without a microwave, but never let it be said that your mother doesn't have determination."

She was supposed to dredge the steak in flour. What the heck was dredging? She flipped through the dictionary which was resting beside the cookbook, ran her finger down the page.

"Oh. Sprinkle or dust with flour before cooking." She eyed the flour as though it were a snake. Every time she tried something that had to do with the contents of that particular canister, it ended in inedible disaster. Even now, the kitchen looked as though it had snowed indoors rather than outside.

But the directions said to dredge, so she dredged, erring on the side of caution with only a light sprinkle.

Through the open window came the sound of horses hooves beating against the ground. And the familiar sound of a truck shifting gears.

She grinned. "Put on your best baby smile, Abbe. Ken's here." The brown UPS truck came up the drive at his usual breakneck speed, regardless of the ground's condition. He made so many trips out here, she was starting to feel as though they were old friends. And since the young man and his wife had a baby of their own, he always stopped to chat, to exclaim over Abbe's growth.

Wiping her hands on her apron, she frowned when the truck stopped short of the front door. Brice had intercepted him by the barn. The two men exchanged greetings, then Ken unloaded a box into the barn, waited for Brice to sign the delivery receipt, then looked toward the house and gave a wave.

Maddie waved back, disappointed when he backed the truck through the open gate of one of the stock pens, then headed out toward the road. She was almost relieved that the order wasn't for her or Abbe—Brice really had gone overboard. But she missed the chance to talk to the friendly young UPS guy.

As she watched his taillights wink in the overcast day, another truck turned down the lane—this one a sport utility driven by Letty Springer.

She recognized the vehicle. Since the wedding, neighbors of the community had been stopping by regularly, regardless of the weather.

And they never came empty-handed. That was hard for Maddie to accept graciously. There were only ten families living along a fifty-mile stretch of roadway, but they were wonderful, caring, giving people who had genuinely accepted Maddie and Abbe into the close-knit community.

Never before had she experienced this feeling of neighborliness. At her rented house in the city, she'd hardly spoken to her neighbors, and they were only a rock's throw away. Still, she couldn't imagine any of the busy acquaintances in Dallas making a special trip to visit or offer help or welcome, yet these people in Wyoming did so without expectations or judgment.

Just acceptance.

She opened the kitchen door and took the casserole dish the woman was balancing along with several other items.

"Hi, Letty."

"Oh, it's cold out there. Snow clouds look like they're going to whip up a blizzard."

"Well, come in and warm up."

"I can only stay a minute. I thought you could use some of this casserole. I made way too much for my family, and with the little one and all, I'm sure you don't have a lot of time." Letty set a jar with about an inch of white goop in the bottom of it on the table and cooed over the baby. "She's growing like a weed."

"The formula agrees with her."

"Yes, it'll fatten her up right quick."

Maddie picked up the jar. "What's this?"

"A starter for Amish friendship bread. And this one's for biscuits." She produced another jar from a paper sack, then laughed at the horrified expression on Madison's face. "Don't worry, hon. I wrote down explicit instructions."

Maddie perused the instructions. There was a ten-day process involved with the bread goop. Day one, do nothing, day two through four stir with a wooden spoon. She glanced at the utensils resting on the stove. Okay. There was one of those in the cow-shaped ceramic holder. Then there was a day of adding ingredients—oh, Lord, flour was one of them—then stirring only for several days, then adding and cooking.

Another thing to baby-sit and possibly mess up. How in the world would she remember which day she'd stirred and which day she'd added? Much less which day to bake. She could barely remember if she combed her hair, much less which day it was.

Maddie didn't have the heart to voice her concerns to Letty.

"What do I do at the part that says divide the batter and give two to friends? By the time I get around to visiting, I'll have a pickup truckload of goop jars."

Letty laughed. "You don't have to give it away. Just double up on the recipe and bake extra loaves. They freeze really well."

Maddie bit her lip, feeling a smile form. "Letty, look around this kitchen, then talk to me again about doubling stuff. I'm a whiz with numbers—unless it has to do with a recipe."

"You'll be just fine. And if you get into trouble, just call. I'll talk you through it."

"Better program your number into my speed dial, then."

"Oh, Madison DeWitt, I *do* like you!"

Maddie got a queer feeling in the pit of her stomach when Letty addressed her by her new surname. She felt like an imposter, felt bad that she was deceiving these wonderful people, but she couldn't bring herself to tell her new friend the story.

The less people who knew, the safer it was for Abbe.

"You okay, hon?"

Maddie nodded and set aside her disturbing thoughts. "Fine. There's one thing I'm bound and determined to master, and that's biscuits. The last batch I attempted came out looking like miniature Frisbees."

"Forgot the baking powder, did you?"

"How did you know?"

"I've done it myself."

"Well, thank goodness. Not that I'm dancing a jig over your biscuits flopping, but knowing I'm not the only one to mess up makes me feel less like an idiot. Can you stay for a few minutes? I'll pour the coffee if you'll give me a crash course in the basics."

"I'll do better than that. I'll make you an expert."

"Letty Springer, you are my angel."

"MIGHTY FINE BISCUITS, Miz Maddie."

"Why thank you, Dan."

"Best chicken-fried steak I've had in a coon's age," Moe added.

Madison laughed. "Now let's not go overboard."

Brice grinned. She was looking proud as a peacock. And well she should. The supper was really good. And personally, he liked a few undercooked lumps in his mashed potatoes.

He'd been stunned when he'd come in to find his house sparkling, the smells of food cooking on the stove, the table set and Madison looking enticing in a pair of jeans with a soft pink sweater tucked in at the waist. Looking at her, no one would think she'd had a baby a month ago.

He had a hard time concentrating.

When Dan and Randy stood to take their plates to the sink, Madison hopped up.

"Don't you dare touch those dishes. That's my job."

"We don't mind," Randy said.

"Shoo. Go play cards or whatever it is you do. I've got it covered. And take the rest of this cake with you."

The ranch hands perked up.

Brice had to object. "Now hold on just a minute. I was hoping for another piece." The utter happiness that came over her face simply arrested him. It was a moment before he could drag his gaze away.

"I'll cut you a piece," she said softly.

He told himself not to read anything into the breathiness of her voice, the look that passed between them.

She was his housekeeper, not really his wife. She was doing her job. That was all.

So why did it feel like the real thing? A family? Why did he suddenly want his ranch hands to get the hell out of here so he could take his wife to bed?

He raked a hand through his hair and stood, avoiding Moe's knowing look as the older man ushered the guys out of the house.

Glasses clinked in the sink as Madison began rinsing the dishes. He moved up beside her, took the plate she'd just scrubbed and put it in the dishwasher.

"You don't have to help."

"I don't mind." Her eyes were strikingly blue tonight, and he wondered if her contact lenses were colored, or if the change was connected to her mood.

"Really, Brice, you've put in a full day. I can do it."

She made an effort to put space between them. Perversely,

he moved right along with her, their bodies brushing. It was torture, but he couldn't seem to help himself. It gave him a punch to realize she was responding to him.

With her hands plunged into a sinkful of water, her hair shifted forward. He reached over and tucked it behind her ear.

She jolted like a skittish filly. "Thank you."

He noticed that her hands were trembling, noticed that his own were none too steady. "I should probably get in there and work on payroll," he said

She drained the water, sprinkled scouring powder in the sink and started to scrub. Her blue eyes held a hint of wariness as she glanced at him. "Uh, I already did that."

"You did?" Figuring out and writing checks was a tedious chore that he hated. It usually took him half the night, and come morning his butt was dragging due to lack of sleep.

"I hope you don't mind. I went back a month and didn't notice any variations in wage rates, so I pretty much just duplicated what you've been doing. It's done except for your signature."

"Did you write yourself a check?"

Her brows drew together as she rinsed the sink. "We agreed that I'm not going to be on the payroll."

"We didn't agree to any such thing."

She shut off the water, turned to face him. "Brice, you've given us your name, a place to live and bought enough baby stuff for three infants instead of just one. You're not paying me a salary."

Before he could argue, Madison reached under the sink and retrieved the plastic bath tub with its sponge insert shaped like a duck.

She bent over to undress the baby, presenting him with her sexy derriere, and he nearly lost his train of thought.

"Last time I checked, I still made the rules around here."

She brushed by him, cooing to the baby, and placed her in

the tub, which rested on the kitchen counter. "Rule all you want outside, but I'm not budging on this issue."

He felt foolish dogging her steps, but the tiny woman wouldn't stay put. He handed her a washcloth. "There's nothing stopping me from writing the check."

"And there's nothing stopping me from tearing it up. Aren't you a sweetheart! You like this bath, don't you?" she cooed.

It took him a moment to realize she was talking to the baby and not him. "Look, sunshine—"

"Watch her for a minute, will you? I forgot to grab a change of clothes."

She didn't give him much choice, just flitted out of the room, leaving him to mind the slippery kid. And feeling frustrated. He was used to getting his way.

But Madison Carlyle—DeWitt, he reminded himself—was turning out to be a worthy opponent, showing the backbone that allowed her to walk a mile and a half in freezing cold, in labor, to deliver a baby without the aid of modern pain medication, to set aside a comfortable life-style and bluff her way into a new one in order to protect her child. A backbone that allowed her to laugh at her mistakes in the kitchen and still keep trying until she got it right.

The backbone to ask a total stranger to marry her.

A damned impressive woman.

Abbe churned her little legs like a frog doing the back stroke, and Brice decided she was clean enough. With his thoughts not wholly on his task, he was likely to drown the kid, never mind that there was only two inches of water in the plastic tub and she was cradled in a formed sponge.

Grinning despite himself, he ran a large palm over her slicked-down hair—not that she had a whole lot of it—and made goofy faces at her. He'd have been embarrassed if anyone caught him in the act. She was a cute thing, with her wide, inquisitive blue eyes and her miniature lips puckered in a circle like an angel fish.

"I'd buy you the moon if you wanted, Abigail DeWitt," he

said softly, feeling his insides turn to mush when he said her name. She was his. For a while.

He wrapped her in a sunny yellow towel until only her round baby face was exposed, then cradled her in the crook of his arm. In that moment he knew he'd move mountains to shield this little girl from harm, deplete all of his vast resources if that's what it took to keep her safe and happy.

The hell of it was, he'd do it for her mother, too.

But in the end what would he get? Probably a Thanks, but see ya.

"If you keep frowning like that, you're going to scare the baby."

Startled, his head whipped up.

"Deep thoughts?"

"Just thinking about business," he lied.

"No wonder. You put in long hours." She took the baby from him, began the efficient steps of diapering and dressing Abbe.

"That's what ranching's all about. On call twenty-four hours a day, seven days a week." There, might as well spell it out, play up the down side of the life he loved, but that most women couldn't endure.

"Mmm, then I imagine you're glad I'm showing a little less ineptitude, so you don't have the burden of the house as well as everything else you do."

He took a prepared bottle out of the refrigerator and set it in a pan of hot water on the stove, barely aware that they were working together like a truly married couple.

"You're doing a good job." And by damn he was going to pay her for the efforts.

"So you've decided to keep me for a while?"

The minute she said the words, they both looked at each other.

For three months.

The time stipulation hung between them like a shout.

Madison turned away first, grabbed the bottle out of the pan, tested its warmth and offered it to the baby.

"Uh, I think I'll finish this up in the nursery. She should fall asleep soon."

He watched her leave the room, felt its emptiness without her presence. The leftover aroma of their evening meal lingered, mingled with the scent of violets and baby talc.

The smell of Madison and Abbe.

The scents he was starting to smell in his dreams.

Hell on fire, he was on really shaky ground here.

WEARING A FLANNEL ROBE belted over thermal pajamas, Maddie stumbled into the kitchen, intent on getting Abbe's bottle before the baby woke up. Her daughter was impatient in the mornings.

For a minute she thought her sleep-fogged brain was playing tricks on her.

Brice leaned against the counter, sipping coffee, his booted feet crossed at the ankles. He wore jeans and a pale green shirt, the ever-present bandanna tied around his neck, but not the chaps she'd gotten used to seeing him in.

It wasn't the sight of all that masculine virility that made her come to a halt as though she'd slammed into a brick wall.

It was the microwave sitting on the counter, with a huge yellow bow tied around it.

She blinked.

The coveted appliance was still there.

"Happy birthday, sunshine," Brice said softly.

Oh, Dear Lord, she was a mess. Tears filled her eyes, spilled over and slid down her cheeks.

He straightened, put down his cup and was in front of her in a heartbeat, his thumbs already brushing at her cheeks.

"What's wrong?"

If she hadn't been so deeply touched, she might have laughed at the bewilderment on his face. She shook her head, glanced again at the microwave.

"How did you know?"

"You mentioned that you were used to using the things and—"

"No." She placed her fingers over his lips, felt her heart beat like a wild thing in her breasts when his eyes flared. "How did you know it was my birthday?"

He cupped her hand, removed it from his mouth so he could talk. "I looked at your driver's license the night I got your car."

Emotions welled up so fast and with such force, she didn't know if she could contain them. A lot of women would be royally ticked at getting a kitchen appliance for their birthday, but Madison was deeply and profoundly touched. He'd chosen the perfect gift, a gift that would make her life easier. She'd relied on herself for so long, and to have someone make things easier for her was a rare treat.

For the first time since she could remember, someone had remembered her birthday. Even she had forgotten—as a way to guard against disappointment, she suspected.

An image flashed in her mind of a little girl getting all dressed up in her finest dress, tying a pink ribbon just so in her hair, fingers crossed, hopes running high, smiling her best smile as she made her way to the dinner table at the foster home. She'd anticipated the surprise, imagined a beautiful doll wrapped in gayly colored paper, or perhaps something more practical, like a nice new pair of wool socks to replace the ones that were worn through with holes. She'd practiced her very best manners, barely containing her excitement as she waited through the dinner of fried chicken and green beans, waited for the part where they'd bring out the cake with seven happy candles glowing.

She'd still been sitting at that trestle table long after the dishes had been done, long after the rest of the family had retired to the living room to watch a television program.

And at the tender age of seven, she'd learned never to hope for too much again.

With his big, rugged hands, Brice cupped her cheeks, gently swiping at the new tears on her cheeks, tipped her face up.

"Hey, there, sunshine. I can return it if it upsets you this much."

She gave a watery laugh. "Touch it and I'll break your fingers."

His grin was so sexy she nearly swooned. "Like it, huh?"

"It's the nicest thing anybody's ever done for me."

"I doubt that."

"No. It truly is. Thank you."

"You're welcome." He looked at her intently, as though he knew about her sadness. "We have a rule on the Flying D. Nobody works on their birthday. What would you say to riding into town with me? You've hardly been out of the house since you've been here."

"I don't mind. And you've done so much for me already."

"Don't start that again. I do what I want. What makes me happy. Besides, I'd appreciate the company."

"All right. I'd like to go with you."

"Nothing spectacular, mind you. I've got to pick up some supplies at the feed store."

"I'd like to go." Hesitating, wondering if she was making a big mistake, she raised up on tiptoe and placed a soft kiss at the corner of his mouth. "Thank you for remembering my birthday."

His hand, which had slipped around her waist, tightened, drawing her closer. She felt his heat, his desire, never even thought about backing away when she saw his head descend, tasted his sweet breath as it mingled with hers.

He was her husband. Surely there wasn't any sin in kissing one's husband.

His lips were firm and sure, speaking of experience and excellence. He smelled of soap, tasted like coffee and hot desire. He shifted, his thigh pressing between her legs, and Maddie was lost. She melted into his embrace, reveled in the gentle way he angled her head, in the heady way he took from her and gave so much more in return. It was a gift, pure and simple.

When he raised his head, she wanted to cling.

His eyes were unreadable. "Happy birthday."

For the life of her she couldn't speak.

He stepped back. "I'll be ready to go when you are."

She was still standing there in a sensual daze as he put his hat on his head and walked out the door.

Lord above, who needed a microwave when they had a man around who could kiss like *that?* She pressed her fingers to her swollen lips.

For that matter, who needed to eat, period?

She heard Abbe's cry from the nursery. Obviously her daughter did.

Chapter Ten

Maddie pulled on the hand-knitted sweater Nancy Adams had just given her. Her birthday was turning into a magical fairy tale, and Madison was feeling like the starring princess.

After their trip to town, Brice had ordered her to rest, then dress in her warmest outfit.

She was both excited and nervous as she came back out of the bedroom. Nancy had agreed to baby-sit, and though Moe tried to act put out that he hadn't been given the sole honor of watching over Abbe, he looked relieved to have the assistance.

"Get, now," Moe said. "I imagine we can handle the little one."

"You have the phone number of where we'll be?" Maddie asked. It was difficult to leave her baby, even though she trusted Nancy and Moe completely. But what if someone showed up, or they got a weird phone call, a subtle clue that the others would miss. A clue that they weren't safe after all, that this was indeed a dream that might soon come to an end.

An end that would mean she'd have to go on the run again.

Brice took her arm. "We're leaving her in good hands, sunshine."

He must have noticed something in her expression. His eyes were concerned. Yet she knew he wouldn't lead her into a situation that would put her in harm's way, or leave the baby if he thought there was an immediate threat.

She nodded, shivered when his fingers brushed her neck as he helped her on with her coat.

"Have fun, you two," Nancy said.

"Thank you, and—"

Brice ushered her out of the house in mid-sentence. Well, honestly. She'd never left her baby before. Nancy might be a nurse, but she didn't know all of Abbe's quirks.

Nor did she know what was really at the root of Maddie's unease.

The icy breeze nearly took her breath away. It was a clear night, with a million stars twinkling, dulled a bit by the full moon shining over the vast expanse of snow-covered ground.

All thoughts of last-minute instructions vanished, and Maddie nearly stumbled when she got a look at the hay wagon that had been retrofitted to double as a sleigh. Two beautiful gleaming horses were harnessed to the vehicle.

It was like something straight out of a fairy tale.

"A sleigh ride?" she said in wonder.

He shrugged, appearing just the slightest bit uncomfortable. "I figured it'd be different."

She was certain her heart was in her eyes, but she didn't care. If this was a dream, she didn't want anyone to wake her.

Brice helped her into the sleigh, placed a blanket over her knees, then picked up the reins and gave a gentle click of his tongue to signal the horses. Jingle bells rang gayly from their harnesses, and Maddie grinned, almost afraid to speak lest she break the enchanted spell.

All around them, snow pillowed on the rooftops of the out-buildings like icing on gingerbread houses. Lit by a bright yellow moon, the distant mountain peaks stood out like stiff meringue on a chocolate cream pie.

"Warm enough?"

"Oh, yes. This is wonderful. Everybody keeps talking about

blizzards, but it hasn't been so bad. The snow is beautiful, magical."

"It's not so magical when you're out working in it."

"I imagine. It's a wonder you don't freeze." She glanced around her, breathing deep of the sweet, bracing air. "Are we still on DeWitt land?"

"Yes. Our spread covers forty thousand acres. It's been in the family for generations." The pride in his voice was hard to miss. She glanced at him, knowing she was reading more into *our* than was warranted. It was only a figure of speech.

"Your records indicate that you handle sheep as well as cattle—"

"Shhh." He glanced down at her, the brim of his hat nearly touching her forehead. His smile flashed in the moonlight, and his voice lowered. "If my great granddaddy caught wind of sheep on DeWitt land, he'd come right up out of his grave "

Her laughter spilled out, causing a beautiful elk to lift his head, his majestic antlers absolutely motionless as the sleigh glided past. "Would Gramps object if I asked why?"

Brice winked, causing her heart to flutter.

"Long as we're bad-mouthing the critters and not praising them. Back in 1911, the cattle ranchers and sheep herders went head to head over in Washakie County in what's known around these parts as the Spring Creek Raid. It turned into a shooting match, which Gramps didn't want any part of, but he was still opposed to sheep being raised on the open range. After that, anytime he caught sight of the woolly creatures, he about had a hissy fit."

"But they're so cute. How could anybody not like them?"

"When they ruin your cattle pastures, they don't look so cute."

"But you have them now."

"I've got enough grazing land to handle both herds. Look." He raised a gloved hand, pointing off to the right. A young doe stood in the moonlight, watching their passage.

"Oh, she's beautiful," Maddie whispered. "It's all so pretty. Cold, but pretty."

He adjusted the blanket over her knees, shifted slightly closer. A protective gesture, a gesture that was gentlemanly and innately Brice.

"It must make you so proud to own all this land. I mean, I'm assuming it's all yours with your dad gone and all."

"I've got a brother. The land just wasn't in Kyle's blood like it is in mine. He traded in his horse for a suit and tie. Deals in the high-finance corporate world."

She wrestled with herself over the next question, decided to ask, anyway. "And your mother?"

His hands tightened on the reins, causing the horses to toss their heads in annoyance. Maddie put her gloved hand on his thigh. "I'm sorry. That's none of my business."

He shrugged, once again holding the reins loosely. "Last I heard she was out in Florida—just married husband number five."

"Do you ever see her?"

"Once. At my dad's funeral. She was hoping for a piece of the pie."

"Oh, dear."

"I offered her a settlement. Beyond that, she wasn't interested in family reunions."

He was quiet for a long time, and Maddie didn't intrude. Besides, the silence felt good, not strained. And she was determined to enjoy every minute of this fanciful trip.

"Where are we going?"

"No place fancy. Just to Laurie's Café in town. Taking the back way like this is quicker."

"And much more scenic." She placed her hand on his arm. "Thank you, Brice. This is wonderful.

He moved the reins slightly to the right and the horses responded immediately, turning. "We're here."

Maddie looked up and felt her heart leap in giddy wonder.

The restaurant was an old Victorian house on the main street in town that had been converted into an inn.

With icy-white covering the land, it didn't look in the least ordinary. In fact, the small strip of shops surrounding Laurie's Café looked like a fanciful row of gingerbread houses. Snow sat on the two-story rooftop like a fluffy cloud, and icicles hung from the gables and eaves. Lights shone in bright welcome as wood smoke curled from the chimney. There were a couple of snowmobiles parked between the buildings, another sleigh and snowshoes were stacked on the wide porch that wrapped around three sides.

"The food's not fancy, but Laurie makes the best desserts around."

"Just what I need. My waistline's still recovering."

He tied the reins around the front of the sleigh, stepped down and reached for her, his hands spanning the waist in question.

Slowly, deliberately it seemed, he lifted her from the sleigh, the front of their bodies brushing. There was no excuse for the way her body responded to his touch, especially with thick layers of winter clothing between them.

But respond it did. Their mingled breaths puffed a visible cloud in the frigid air. He held her suspended for several seconds at eye level. She gripped his shoulders, unable to look away from the sensual promise in his gaze.

"Your waistline feels just fine to me," he murmured, his voice whisky smooth and filled with sexual innuendo.

She wondered if a heart could actually stand still. In a strange sort of daze, she realized that his breath was the only one creating steam.

"Breathe," he coached, then covered her mouth with his. His lips were cold, yet they scorched a path of fire through her. He lowered her slowly along the length of his body until her feet touched the ground. She had an irrational urge to cling, to beg.

He lifted his head, gently touched her cheek. The smell of fine leather wafted from his gloves.

A snowflake landed on the tip of her nose and she laughed, breaking the spell.

He smiled. "I like it when you laugh. It's nice." He took her arm, steadied her. "Ready to go have your birthday dinner?"

She nodded, even though she could have skipped dinner and just spent the evening looking at him under the light of a full moon with the fairy stars twinkling overhead and the horses' harnesses jingling behind them.

Laurie met them at the door and beamed. "I'm so glad you called, Brice, it's been forever since you've been here."

Brice leaned down and accepted the friendly kiss Laurie placed on his cheek, then straightened and extended his hand to Jerome, who'd come out of the kitchen wearing a white chef's apron.

"I've been cooking all day just for you and your bride," Jerome said.

Madison felt a little awkward. She glanced around the interior. There were five other couples in the quaint dining room. A stone hearth hugged the corner wall, and a fire crackled invitingly. The smell of garlic and herbs vied with the pine logs burning in the grate and the scented candles on the white tablecloths. Shadow boxes, flower boughs and decoupage plaques covered the pastel walls, giving the place the feel of a craft store rather than an inn. The floors were wood plank, and around the corner through an archway, was a gift shop with a potpourri of souvenirs and antiques.

The place was homey rather than fancy, and Maddie was enchanted.

"May I take your coat, Mrs. DeWitt?"

"Uh, please, call me Maddie." She glanced at Brice to see how he reacted to people calling her by his name. He was busy shucking his outer gear, had his back turned. She slipped out of her own coat and gloves, unwound the scarf from her neck.

"Shall I take your hat?" Laurie asked him.

He removed the black Stetson, but kept it with him, grinning.

"I promise not to wear it at dinner, but I think I'll hang on to it if it's all the same to you."

"Oh, you cowboys and your hats," Laurie admonished. "Suit yourself. Come, I'll show you to your table."

There were sprigs of fresh daisies, lilacs and carnations in a crystal vase in the center of their table. A white card with Madison's name on it stuck out of the arrangement, clasped by a plastic florist's fork. She glanced around at the other tables, noticed that this one was the only one with a bouquet of fresh flowers—the others had silk arrangements in ginger jars.

She wanted to reach out and touch, but was ridiculously afraid it would vanish.

Brice held her chair, waited until she sat, then settled across from her. "You can read the card."

Her fingers actually trembled as she plucked the envelope out of its holder and slowly withdrew the card.

The message was simple. "Happy Birthday, Madison." Signed with Brice's name. No salutation of love, but that didn't matter.

She fought back the misting in her eyes, cleared her throat. "Thank you."

"You're welcome."

"How did you manage fresh flowers way out here—in the dead of winter?"

He grinned. "I'm fairly acquainted with the delivery people around these parts."

She bit her lower lip, drummed her fingers against the white damask table linen. "I believe that's an understatement."

He uncorked the bottle of champagne that was resting in a silver ice bucket beside the table, poured two glasses and handed her one.

"To birthdays," he toasted.

She touched her goblet to his, took a sip of the bubbly wine. She felt giddy already, drunk on just his company, on the magic of the night. It was more potent than the drink.

"This is a first for me. I've never had a birthday dinner before."

He paused with the goblet halfway to his mouth, then set it back on the table. "Never?"

She shook her head, looked away, wondered why she'd revealed that.

"Did your family not celebrate—for religious reasons?"

"I've had a lot of families over the years, been exposed to a lot of religions. Nobody ever cited religious beliefs for not celebrating." She drummed her fingers on the tabletop, repositioned her napkin. "They probably just didn't know the date of my birthday."

"What about your parents?"

She shrugged, told herself it no longer hurt, that she was a grown woman now, well over the pain. "They gave me away. Actually, my father left and my mother turned me over to social services, signed away all claim to me."

His jaw clenched, as did his fist around the stem of the fine crystal. "And you weren't adopted?"

"People don't adopt big kids. Only little babies."

"That's not true, sunshine."

She fiddled with her fork, swept her hair behind her ear. "Seemed that way in my case. There were kids who'd lost their folks to tragedies. Some of them found permanent homes. I guess they figured if my parents gave me away, there must be a reason."

"Damn," he said softly, and reached across the table, covering her hand, putting a halt to her nervous drumming. She tried to draw back, but he tightened his hold. "That's not pity, sunshine, so tuck your chin back down. Just makes me mad, is all."

Her hand relaxed in his. She turned her palm up, linked their fingers. "I always feel compelled to say thanks to you. You're a good man, Brice DeWitt."

His fingers tightened over hers, his intense gaze holding

her. Eyes the color of a deep lake reflected the flickering of the candle, the intensity of swift and immediate desire.

Snagged by the heat of his gaze, Maddie couldn't look away. Silverware scraped against china, and voices droned, blending with the occasional laugh. Someone opened the front door, letting in a blast of cold air.

But all Maddie could feel was heat as an odd trembling raced just beneath her skin, humming through her blood as though charged by electricity.

The atmosphere in the room seemed to shift, to narrow, to encompass just the two of them. The moment spun out, a moment that should have been conducted in private, behind closed doors.

Her imagination took off on that scenario, picturing the two of them, the textures, the flavors, the differences in their bodies, soft to hard...

"Keep looking at me like that and I'm liable to forget my civilized manners."

His voice was low and as rough as a splintery board. And it sent her heart into a frenzy. Dear Lord, what would it be like to have him unleash all that provocative sexuality? To have his whole attention focused on just her?

She reached for her water glass and turned her gaze to the decorative crafts on the wall.

"Smart woman," he murmured.

Her gaze shot back to him, and for the life of her she couldn't help pushing him a bit, playing the game. She was rusty with the social skills practiced between men and woman, but perversely she was willing to give it a shot.

"You strike me as a man who rarely loses control. I really doubt you could act uncivilized." At least not in public. It was those darn private images that were so enticing.

His brows arched. "There are those who would disagree with you."

"Oh?" She grinned. "Do I detect a hell-raiser lurking beneath the laid-back-cowboy veneer?"

One corner of his mouth canted in amusement. "I've been in a brawl or two."

She shook her head. "I can't imagine you busting up furniture and stuff."

Now he was the one fiddling with the utensils, looking sheepish. "It's rough on the checkbook."

"I was kidding," she said. "But you're not. You actually damaged furniture?"

"A few bar tables, a couple of mirrors."

"Hopefully you're not superstitious."

"Seven years, bad luck?"

"Fourteen if it was two mirrors."

"Guess I've only got eight years to go, then."

She grinned. "Hardly. From the looks of your accounts, you've had nothing but *good* luck. Your ranch is very prosperous. And speaking of prosperous, I've been meaning to ask you about the price you've paid for a couple of bulls. My eyes nearly bugged out. Are you sure you've shopped around for the best deal?"

He leaned back in his chair and laughed, making her stare. His face relaxed, and if she'd thought he was merely handsome before, now she couldn't quite find the word for him. His white shirt fit the breadth of his chest as though tailor-made for his measurements. A red silk bandanna was tied around his neck. Firelight shimmered off his dark hair, playing over his sculpted cheekbones, his square jaw, his sensual lips that could grin like the brightest sun or kiss the very daylights out of her.

She took a gulp of champagne, licked her bottom lip.

His smile faltered, his gaze sharpening. He cleared his throat.

"I'm one of the toughest bargainers around. I got those bulls at rock-bottom prices."

"Good heavens, why would you want something that expensive?"

"To ensure the quality of my stock. You of all people should understand the concept of artificial insemination."

She'd managed to go quite a while without thinking about the pall that hung over her life, the threat to her child. With one simple statement, it all came slamming back.

"Aw, sunshine, I didn't think."

She pulled her thoughts back from the precipice. "It's okay. My reasons weren't based on quality of stock. I didn't want to know his name or anything about him. I just knew my baby would be special because she was mine, regardless of pedigree."

He winked to lighten the mood. "Well, she's got your genes, so she comes from good stock."

Laurie came out and placed a steaming basket of fresh bread on the table, along with plates of chicken and homemade noodles. "Enjoy, you two."

The meal smelled wonderful, but Maddie frowned. "Did you order ahead of time?" she asked.

"No. Each night there's a special and that's what you get. Like I said, it's not fancy."

It almost sounded as though he was apologizing for the place. She could have told him it wasn't necessary. To her, the special touches of flowers and champagne made her feel like she was in the richest five-star restaurant.

The chicken was so tender she could cut it with her fork. "Isn't it sacrilegious or something not to eat beef in cattle country?"

He grinned. "Wednesday and Thursday are fish and chicken. The rest of the week is beef. Your birthday happened to fall on chicken night."

"Well, I'm glad—not to malign your industry or anything. But this is the best meal I've had in longer than I remember." Certainly since she'd been doing the cooking.

"Don't get out much, do you?"

"I keep pretty busy. There was so much to do getting ready for the baby and setting up my house and the business. My dining experiences ran more toward fast-food takeout." She smiled. "Or microwave dinners."

He gave a pained expression.

"Now don't you go regretting my new appliance. I promise not to feed you guys TV dinners."

"You'd surely have a revolt on your hands."

Two musicians dressed in Western-cut suits took their places by the fire and adjusted microphones. Soon the dining room was filled with the combination of guitar and fiddle music. Maddie listened to the song about riding across prairies and a cowboy's lament over losing his girl. When the older of the two entertainers went into a gentle yodeling rendition, Maddie laid down her fork and clapped along with the rest of the customers.

She glanced at Brice, noticing that he was watching her instead of the entertainment.

"What?" she asked.

"Nothing."

Brice couldn't seem to tear his eyes away from the animation on her face. Everything seemed to delight her, and that made him feel good. Her enjoyment was genuine.

Sharon had thought yodeling was silly and backward. And he couldn't remember his ex-wife ever giving a thought to the bulls he bought. It surprised him how much Madison's interest in what he did pleased him.

When Laurie came to clear their plates, he shifted his chair closer to Madison's so they could watch the entertainers. At least that's what he told himself. More and more lately, he found himself wanting to be close, to touch, to smell, to taste.

To dream.

He was on dangerous ground, and he knew it. But he couldn't seem to help himself.

When the song ended, Madison clapped louder than anyone else in the room. The guitar player spoke into the microphone.

"Thank you kindly, folks. I'm Clarence, and this here's my brother Eugene. We'll be playing some slow dancin' music for your listening and dancing pleasure, but first, it's come to our attention that there's a birthday in the house tonight. Why don't you all join us in singing to Miz Madison DeWitt."

Madison's head whipped around so fast, her hair smacked Brice across the face. "You didn't!"

He tried to act innocent, but failed. Actually, he was still trying to get his heart rate to settle after hearing her addressed as DeWitt. "It was Laurie's doing."

"But you told her."

"Yeah, I did. Now hush up and listen as everybody sings to you."

Her cheeks were rosy with pleasure, and he was glad he'd told Laurie what they were celebrating. Madison deserved this. Another first, he realized.

Laurie and Jerome carried out a birthday cake blazing with candles and set it on the table as the whole room sang.

And though obviously not used to the attention, Madison was a good sport about it, standing when the song was over and taking a bow as the customers clapped.

"I can't believe you did that," she said when she sat back down.

With his arm across the back of her chair, he toyed with her hair. "Admit it, sunshine. You're glad I did."

She nodded, and for a minute there, he thought she was going to cry. Candle wax was melting on the buttercream frosting.

"Make a wish," he said softly.

She closed her eyes, giving the impression that she was thinking long and hard. Something shifted inside him, a softness around his heart, as he watched her. To go twenty-nine years without somebody making a fuss over your birthday was so sad. She leaned forward, managed all the candles with one puff, then ducked her head when more clapping ensued.

"How about a birthday dance?" Clarence said into the microphone, then strummed his guitar softly. Someone dimmed the lights in the room.

Brice started to stand, but Maddie slapped a hand on his thigh. "Oh, no. I haven't danced in ages. I'm really rusty."

He took her hand in his, rose despite her objections and pulled her to her feet. "Then it's about time we remedied that."

He led her to a corner of the room that had been cleared for dancing, and pulled her into his arms. Compared to him she felt tiny and he couldn't help but grin when he noticed that she stood on tiptoe. Normally he found dancing with short women didn't work well.

With Madison, it felt like a perfect fit.

"If I stomp on your feet, don't say I didn't warn you," she whispered.

"These boots have been stomped on before. Relax."

Maddie tried to relax, but it was difficult. She was in the arms of the most handsome man around. Her husband. In front of an audience.

The muscles of his shoulders shifted beneath her hand. His heat burned her, made her want, made her forget that they were the only couple on the dance floor with a roomful of folks looking on. She felt his lips brush her temple, felt his palm at her back urge her even closer.

Nancy Adams's words came back to her— *Some women are ready in two weeks, claim their hormones have gone haywire.*

Well, Maddie could attest to haywire hormones. Hers were all but standing on end, begging to be set free.

Usually her instincts were to think the situation to death, to list the pros and cons, to make sure everything was in balance, to consider the bottom line.

But those instincts were obviously on vacation tonight.

Because tonight all she wanted to do was feel, to go with the emotions, to see just where they would lead.

She tipped her head back, looked into his eyes, tried desperately to read his expression.

The love she felt for him swelled, pounded through her veins.

She wanted a real marriage with this man, wanted the world to stand still, to wrap them in a blanket of security, wanted to forget every worry, every threat, every outside intrusion.

"You're doing it again," he said quietly, a muscle working in his jaw.

"Doing what?"

"Looking at me in a way that's testing my civilized manners."

She licked her lips. "I don't recall ever asking you to be civilized."

His eyes flared and his palm tightened against hers. "Careful, sunshine. I'm trying to remember that you've just had a baby."

"Over four weeks ago."

"Hell," he muttered and gently pressed her face to his neck. "You make me forget my own name. Whatever you do, when the music stops, just keep dancing."

She felt his body's response to her, felt a heady sense of feminine power that she could affect him so, knew that if they stepped apart, anybody who cared to look would see his body's reaction, too.

"And what happens when the band takes a break?"

"Hush. I'm counting."

She grinned, and perversely pressed closer.

He groaned. "Now I've lost my place."

"What are you counting?"

"Cattle."

A bubble of laughter tickled her insides. "Should I be insulted?"

He exhaled a long breath. "You're determined to distract me, aren't you."

"Yes," she admitted honestly, boldly.

He leaned back, met her gaze. She wasn't good at this sort of thing, was probably making a hash of it.

But it somehow felt right.

She wanted him. She loved him. He was her husband.

The final notes of the guitar faded away. He turned her around, walked behind her to the table and grabbed his hat.

"We'll take the cake to go."

Chapter Eleven

Maddie was certain her frayed nerves and thoughts were emblazoned across her forehead as she let herself into the house. Brice was still outside, tending to the horses.

"Did you enjoy yourself?" Nancy asked, rising from the sofa and hitting the Remote button to turn off the television.

"Yes." Major understatement. "How was Abbe?"

"A perfect angel."

Maddie smiled. "Cried a bit, did she?"

"Nope," Moe said, coming out of the kitchen. "Little girlie slept the whole dang evenin'." The older man looked so forlorn that Maddie laughed.

"I appreciate the two of you keeping her for me."

"That's what friends are for." Nancy hugged Maddie and kissed her cheek. "Will we see you in church Sunday?"

Maddie nodded, surprised by the warm hug, the support. These people were amazing.

"Okay. Call if you need anything in the meantime." The nurse gathered up her coat and keys and let herself out the door.

"Guess I'll turn in, too," Moe said. "Happy birthday, missy."

"Thank you, Moe. It's been the best ever."

"That's the way it's s'posed to be."

Alone in the house, Maddie went to check on Abbe, who was indeed sleeping like an angel. She adjusted the blanket, smoothed a hand over the baby's downy soft head, wishing her daughter would wake up.

Now that she'd all but propositioned Brice, she was suddenly nervous.

What now? Should she change clothes? Put on something sexy? She nearly laughed out loud. She didn't own anything sexier than a floor-length flannel gown.

Should she wait in the bedroom? In the living room? Or should she act casual, heat a cup of chocolate in her new microwave?

She went to the bedroom, stood in the middle of the room, stared at the bed.

Brice's bed.

For heaven's sake! She wasn't a virgin. Yet she felt more high-strung than one.

Casual, she decided. She'd go make that chocolate, take her cue from Brice when he came in. For all she knew, he'd changed his mind—or worse, she'd misread his signals.

She turned and nearly screamed.

He stood in the doorway, hat brushing the top of the jamb, shoulder resting against the wood, watching her.

She licked her lips, laced her fingers together.

Casual.

"I'm not sure what to do." She closed her eyes. So much for casual, she chided silently.

She felt his fingers touch her chin, cold from being outdoors, smelled the tangy scent of his aftershave mingling lightly with the earthy scent of horses. For such a big man, he moved so silently.

"We don't have to do this, you know."

She opened her eyes, looked up at him. Desire was there, and it was mutual. It gave her courage.

"I think we do. Or at least, *I* do. There's snow on the ground outside, but I'm burning up."

He kissed her then, spoke against her lips. "You can't imagine what your honesty does to me." He held her close, his hands stroking a path of fire across her back. "Do you feel it?"

"Yes."

"Be sure, sunshine."

"I'm sure."

"It's been a while for me."

"Me, too."

"Yes, but I'm not sure I can be gentle, be what you need. Frankly, I'm scared to death."

"Then you're in good company. My insides are shaking like mad. But Nancy said it was…um, okay to do it."

He went stock-still, astonished. "You *asked* her?"

She giggled, stunned by the sound. She rarely did such a thing. "No. She volunteered that permission when she, uh, examined me last."

"In that case…" With his lips pressed to hers, he walked her backward toward the bed, then combed his fingers through her hair, looked at her for a long moment as though battling with some inner demon.

"This doesn't change anything. Our three-month agreement still stands."

It almost sounded like a question. But his true emotions were firmly hidden.

Her heart stung. She ducked her head so he wouldn't see the hurt, and nodded.

For just an instant his hands tightened on her shoulders, then gentled. "I didn't mean that the way it sounded. You've been through so much, the last thing I want is to make you feel trapped, obligated in any way."

There was compassion in his voice, and a hint of sadness that both surprised and touched her. "I don't feel trapped with you, Brice. I feel so much, so full—"

He stopped her words with his lips, as though he were a man about to lose his tenuous control. Yet his hands were incredibly gentle as he undressed her, then himself, lowered her to the bed and followed.

"Tell me what you like."

"I don't know." She hadn't been kidding when she'd said it had been a long time for her.

"Then we'll play it by feel, make it up as we go along."

And oh, he was an expert at it. For what seemed like hours, he simply kissed her, caressed her, worshiped her. He stroked her body, arousing her with the mere tips of his fingers, so slowly, so reverently, so thoroughly.

The experience was nothing short of exquisite. There was no rush for final completion. In fact, his fingers skipped over the very places she ached most for his touch, teasing her, setting her on fire.

He gave the impression of having all the patience in the world, setting a pace that nearly drove her mad.

Unaccountably she felt tears back up as need built, hot and explosive.

"Touch me, please." Her breath hitched when his palm mapped the length of her inner thigh, skimmed, teased. The anticipation was pure, sensual torture.

"I am," he said, sketching her jaw with his lips.

"I mean…more." Couldn't he see that she was on fire?

"I don't want to hurt you."

"You won't." She reached for his hand, pressed it to her. And with that barest touch, she came apart, could have sworn she actually screamed. In the maelstrom of powerful sensations, there was a moment of clarity, a flash of embarrassment.

This was the second time she'd screamed in his bed. At least she hadn't ripped the sheets this time.

"You are so responsive, sunshine. I want you."

"You have me."

Brice couldn't believe how those three words pierced his heart. He didn't really have her. She was only temporary.

But reality was impossible to dwell on now. The want was too strong, the need too consuming.

With gazes locked, he entered her, slowly, watching for any

sign of discomfort, sweat trickling down his temples as he held on to his control by a single thread.

The experience was so new to him. He hadn't known the patience was there, hadn't known his senses could be so acute. With the utter slowness of their joining, the total focus of his concentration on her pleasure, awareness sharpened. A sense of déjà vu stole over him, as though he'd known her all his life, touched her just like this, looked at her just like this, felt her warmth close around him just like this.

Moonlight shone in the window, bathed her skin in its glow. He saw the faint trace of blue veins on her swollen breasts, felt the pebble of her nipples brush his chest.

Her eyes, open and locked on to his, were filled with wonder…and utter trust.

She reached out and touched his cheek, shattering something inside him.

Good intentions and vows of gentleness vanished. He was helpless to stop the building tide, the momentum.

Maddie gripped his shoulders, unable to hold on to any single sensation for more than a second. The very air around them shimmered as desire coiled in her belly, dark and desperate.

She wanted to beg, but didn't know what to beg for. She wanted to slow down, to savor, yet she couldn't get enough, couldn't seem to go fast enough.

She felt a sob building, felt poised on the very brink of discovery, on the incendiary edges of the brightest, most exquisite star in the heavens.

The sensations snatched her breath, rolled over her. Her skin was slick with perspiration, her breasts sensitive to the point of pain.

"Stay with me," he coached.

And just that quickly the dam of emotions burst, flooding her with mind-numbing pleasure that frightened even as it thrilled, sensations that rushed her headlong into another stunning climax.

She cried out his name, knowing he would answer, that he would hold her, catch her, break her fall.

Knowing that the love she felt would burn in her heart for the rest of her life.

WHEN MADDIE WOKE, she was alone. Snowflakes drifted past the window. Brice would have a cold day out on the range. She tried not to feel hurt that he wasn't there to hold her, to kiss her awake.

But he had work to do. And so did she.

She had a husband and home to take care of. She didn't dare think about what would happen if the Covingtons should find her, promised herself she wouldn't think past each day, would take life as it came.

Brice's words echoed, stinging anew. *This doesn't change anything.* She'd already used up a month of her stay. And for a woman who liked to have her future planned right down to the day, her life was far too uncertain.

She set aside those thoughts and went to check on the baby. It was still early, yet she wondered if Abbe had cried during the night and maybe she hadn't heard her. She also wondered if Brice had ever placed that order for baby monitors.

Tying the belt of her robe, she went into the nursery and stopped in her tracks.

Brice was dressed and standing by the side of the crib, staring down at the baby—who was still sleeping.

As though he sensed her presence, he turned his head, met her gaze. For an instant there was naked need in his dark blue eyes, a starkness to his handsome features.

She wasn't sure how to act. Her hands tugged at the tie of her robe, nearly cutting off her air.

"Morning," he said softly, then moved away from the crib, coming toward her. "I was just checking on the baby."

"Me, too." What an inane conversation. She wanted to put her arms around him, tell him she loved him, beg him to tell her how he felt, to let her know if last night had affected him as profoundly as it had her.

To assure her that nobody could ever take her baby from her.

To promise her longer than three months.

He lifted his hand as though to touch her, closed his fingers into his palm. "You okay?"

"Fine."

He nodded. "I better get to work."

"I should fix you breakfast."

"I'll grab something later."

They were acting like strangers, but for the life of her, she didn't know how to change the mood. She wasn't one to deliberately set herself up for rejection. And to push an issue was a surefire way of showing her vulnerabilities, of having those vulnerabilities exploited.

In the end, she took the coward's way out and simply watched him walk away.

STRAPPING ABBE into her infant seat, Maddie set the baby in the middle of the kitchen table and heated a cup of water for tea in her new microwave.

Well, it wasn't actually hers. When she left, the appliance would stay—it wouldn't fit in her car. But she didn't want to think about leaving. She looked around the room, feeling different, more territorial about the house after last night.

As though this were really her home.

And home was what she yearned for.

The jar of bread paste that she'd diligently stirred, added to and watched like a hawk was hidden behind an open cookbook. According to the instructions, there was one more stirring day and it would be time to bake.

She moved the cookbook and nearly screamed in frustration. The darn mixture had tripled in size, oozing over the sides of the jar. She snatched up a rag, wiped the mess and reread the instructions, certain she'd done everything Letty had told her. Had she missed a day giving it a stir?

Good Lord, couldn't she get anything right? Admonishing herself to calm down, she poured the batter into a larger jar, sorely tempted to try baking a loaf, but resisted. The rules said it wasn't time, and she was a stickler for rules.

But come tomorrow she would bake a loaf of sweet bread if it killed her.

Hopefully it wouldn't kill the men!

She worked on Brice's accounting, waxed the furniture, kept the fire stoked and stared at the clothes dryer, determined to catch the cycle the minute it finished. The ironing board was already set up and waiting. She'd been keeping an eye on the barn throughout the morning and knew the guys were still around. They'd be wanting lunch before long, and she intended to surprise them with a plate of sandwiches.

The dryer buzzed and she took out the clothes, transferred them to the table by the ironing board.

She hesitated over Brice's jeans, then shrugged, lining the seams up and pressing a smart crease down the center. If that was wrong, at least she could fix the error and iron it out. Not like cutting off the hem and making them flood pants.

Abbe napped on and off throughout the morning. She fed the baby, dressed her warmly, then packed up the sandwiches.

She was trying to figure out how to manage food and the baby when Brice came through the back door.

She whirled around, stared at him.

Once again, the silence seemed strained. Get over it, she told herself. The morning after had passed. It was noon.

She took a breath, steadied her nerves. "I made lunch. I was just about to bring it out to you guys." He was wearing woollies over his jeans today, chaps made out of thick fleece. Buckled low on his waist, and tied around his inner thighs, they were sexy as all get-out and made her fantasies stand up and take notice.

He toyed with the brim of his hat, then removed his gloves.

"You don't have to bring lunch out. It's too cold out there, anyway."

"I don't mind. And you all must be hungry."

Yes, Brice thought. He was hungry. But not for lunch. She wore a pair of formfitting jeans and a soft white sweater that made him want to reach out and touch, to stroke the gentle curve of her breasts. Now that she wasn't nursing the baby, her breasts weren't as large, but she still had the sexiest curves—and in all the right places.

He forced himself to look away from temptation. "I'll call down to the barn, have the men come to the house."

"You can do that?"

"Do what?"

"Call the barn."

"Yes. I should have given you the number. I wasn't thinking."

He picked up the phone, and his mind went blank. He'd been dialing that number half his life, and he couldn't even remember the first few digits.

"Brice?"

Her tone had him hesitating, turning back to her. "Yeah?"

"I won't bite."

He frowned. "What's that supposed to mean?"

"You're avoiding me. Because of last night."

He hung up the phone without dialing, raked a hand through his hair. "I'm not used to sleeping with my housekeeper." She winced and he felt like a jerk. That hadn't come out right.

"I'd like to think I'm more than that," she said softly. "I'd like to think that we're at least friends."

"Sunshine, what we did last night was a hell of a lot more than friendship."

"True. But we're both adults. Consenting adults."

"Are you saying you're willing to have an affair?"

She shrugged, didn't quite meet his eyes. "According to the State of Wyoming, we *are* married."

"But you and I know the reason for that marriage."

She turned, fussed with a dishrag, then took a deep breath. "Never mind."

He went to her, touched her shoulder, felt her stiffen. "No, get it off your chest."

"We're acting like two teenagers who've done something wrong. We're living under the same roof. I just thought we should deal with the discomfort, get past it."

He turned her to face him. "I don't want to take advantage of you."

"I'm a big girl. And it's not taking advantage if I give you permission."

His fingertips traced her soft cheek, and his chest swelled with emotion. If he wasn't concerned about one of the men walking in, he'd take her right here in the kitchen. Because phony marriage or not, he wanted her with a burning fire that consumed him.

"Just don't treat me like a stranger," she pleaded.

He cupped the back of her head, pulled her to him and kissed her. Her mouth opened and her hands gripped his shoulders. He pressed her against him, reveling in the beat of her heart, in the pounding of his own.

Lifting his head, he said, "Does that feel like a stranger to you?"

"Your lips feel familiar. I can't say the same for those strange animal skins on your legs." Her voice trembled, and he wasn't sure if it was from laughter or desire.

When he saw the amusement dancing in her expressive blue eyes, he couldn't stop the smile that tugged at his lips. "Makes me look a little like a beast, hum?"

She laughed. "Quit. You're going to give me inappropriate ideas."

Desire, swift and incendiary, swept through him. "If you give me five minutes to make sure the guys are occupied, I'd like to hear about that fantasy you're conjuring up."

Her face flamed and she ducked her head, thumped him on the chest. "It's the middle of the day."

"So? Haven't you ever made love at lunchtime before?"

"As a matter of fact, no."

That stunned him. She was a passionate woman. "Never?"

She shook her head, and he believed her. The baby fussed, reminding him that now was not the time to get carried away. But soon, he promised himself, he was going to show this woman the merits of making love in the bright light of day.

He tightened his arm around her, allowed the thick, fleecy chaps to press against her, to tease.

"Oh!" she breathed, her chest rising and falling, sorely testing his good intentions as her breasts brushed against him.

He loved that little catch in her voice, the way her eyes went round in wonder. This was a woman who wasn't coy, who wasn't afraid of trying new experiences.

That was evident by her answering a job advertisement when she hadn't known the first thing about ranching or cooking.

But she had a keen interest in his life-style and a determination to learn, to experiment. She was a good sport. He wanted to test her limits, reap the benefits of her enthusiasm.

Tired of being ignored, Abbe let out a shriek.

Brice stepped back, went over to the table. "Hey there, little girl. What's the fuss?"

The sound of his voice made her little eyes round.

Maddie cleared her throat. "Could you take her out of the seat and hold her for a minute until I get a bottle fixed?"

"I'm pretty dirty. Why don't you get her and I'll heat the milk." Each time he held the baby, he fell a little deeper in love.

Just like every time he held her mother, he fell a little deeper...in what? He didn't want to finish that thought.

"Not on your life," Maddie said. "I intend to play with that microwave every chance I get. Besides, Abbe won't mind a bit of dirt. Plus it'll get her used to the scents of the ranch. These are things little girls should know."

There was no reason those simple, offhand words should give him such pleasure, but they did. He yearned for a family who'd embrace the ranch and land as he did. But hope was a dangerous thing, and he tried to quell it.

Obeying her directive, he took the baby out of the seat. "Uh-oh. She's pretty wet." Now that he had the infant in his arms, he was reluctant to give her up so soon. "I'll go see if I can muddle through a diaper change. Come rescue us if you hear major screaming."

"Yours or hers?"

"Cute."

Maddie smiled and watched him carry the baby out of the room. He was a fantasy man. Giving gifts, making things easier on her, taking care of the baby.

A man so easy to love. Yet he still held such a big part of himself back, guarded his emotions like a child guards a coveted toy.

She placed a bottle in the microwave, set the timer for fifteen seconds.

Through the kitchen window, she saw a flash of brown against the pristine white of snow.

Ken, the UPS guy, was out with another delivery.

What now? She chuckled and went to the front door to meet him, pulling open the door and stepping out onto the porch. The sun was shining, and the snow on the ground nearly blinded her, causing her eyes to water. Without a coat, she shivered a bit, but drew in a deep breath of crisp air that smelled of wood smoke and animals—scents that were becoming so familiar, so comforting.

Expecting just Ken, her heart thudded for no reason when she noticed the other man in the passenger seat of the step-side van. Her hands trembled, and for a moment she wanted to turn, to charge back in the house and slam the door, to lock it against strangers, against an eerie feeling that was totally un-grounded.

Don't be stupid, she chided herself. The man with Ken wore the standard brown uniform, looked perfectly innocent.

"It's customers like you who make my day," Ken said

brightly, holding out a clipboard as his partner held a small shipping carton.

Maddie still stared at the new man.

Ken noticed. "This is Darrell," he introduced. "New man on the job. I'm training him, and he's getting a baptism by ice with all the cold weather and slippery roads. Good thing you're on the snowplow's route."

"The guys here keep the roads cleared," she said absently, accepting the clipboard. She heard the front door open and turned when Brice stepped out on the porch, carrying the baby.

Her gaze darted to the trainee, then back to Brice and her daughter. Irrationally she wanted to grab Abbe and run. Brice had wrapped the baby in a blue blanket and had the ends pulled over her face to guard against the cold.

Maddie abandoned the clipboard and scooped Abbe right out of his arms, not even giving Ken his usual chance to coo over her.

"It's cold out here. I'll take the baby back inside. You go ahead and sign. Good seeing you again, Ken."

She was in the house before anyone could ask questions, holding her daughter to her breast, breathing deep.

A moment later Brice came in.

"You okay, sunshine?"

"Fine."

He touched her pale cheek, not liking that fragile look in her eyes. She had the look of an angel who'd just gotten a devastatingly vivid glimpse of hell.

"You're not fine. Sit before you fall." Despite her protests, he plucked the baby out of her arms and ushered her to the sofa. "What was all that about?"

He saw her close her eyes, gather her control. "I hadn't expected Ken to have anyone with him."

"You're thinking about private investigators again?"

She gave him a defiant look. "Yes."

"I don't think the UPS guy would go along with that."

"Well, I don't imagine a snoop's gonna announce his intentions. That's what they do, skulk around, blend in with people in order to get their information."

"Either you've been watching too much TV, or I've been out of touch. I think you're overreacting." He raised his hand when she started to light into him. "Don't get me wrong. I'm not discounting your worries. But from all you've told me, you've covered your tracks really well. Have you used a credit card since you left?"

"No."

"Made any bank transactions or anything else traceable?"

"Just giving birth to Abbe, and that's under your name, not mine."

He glanced down at the baby. Yes, she had his name, by God. And she was really starting to feel like his.

"I'll have my attorney make some inquiries, if you like. Find out what legal ramifications can arise if the Covingtons do find you. I'm no lawyer, but I don't think the sperm donor's parents have any rights. You're a good mother, sunshine. They'd have to prove otherwise in order to have a legal leg to stand on."

"I've seen the system fail plenty of times. All you have to do is turn on the news and you're bound to see somebody's pain and suffering. That's what scares me. Even if I have right on my side, what if something goes wrong? That's the small percentage that I'm not willing to chance."

No, he wasn't either, if truth be told. He shifted the baby along his arm, cradled her head, a corner of his brain registering the fact that he was getting pretty good at holding and changing and feeding this tiny girl.

He moved to the sofa, sat and put his free arm around Madison, pulling her to his side. It felt right, sitting here by the fire, the three of them snuggled together like a real family.

A real family that he desperately wanted.

But whether he could have them for keeps or not, he knew one thing for certain. He would protect these two females with his life.

"I won't let anyone hurt you, sunshine. You have my promise."

Madison snuggled into his side, placing her hand over his, which rested atop the fluffy blue blanket, creating a circle. A family circle.

Oh, man. He wanted to protect her from the Covingtons, had in essence promised her that all would be well, that she would never lose Abbe.

But he was scared to death.

That eerie sense of expectancy was nagging at him again. That same sensation he'd felt just before Madison had shown up at his door, before his life had been forever altered by this tiny woman and her sweet baby.

The sweet baby who now bore his name.

God, he'd failed so many times in his life—failed to keep his mom from leaving, failed to keep his dad alive, failed to keep Sharon from leaving.

He wanted it to be different this time.

Wanted to try. For Madison.

Chapter Twelve

Brice had just finished putting Samson away after a freezing-cold ride to break up the ice and keep the water flowing in the creek, and he still had a full day ahead of him.

He came out of the barn, a rope in his hand to corral a weak cow, and stopped when he saw Madison trudging through the snow toward him. She had her purse slung over her shoulder, carried the cumbersome infant seat in one hand and a covered dish in another. She looked like a woman on a mission, and for a minute, all he could do was stare, arrested by the sight of her in that flimsy coat with its absurd fur around the collar.

If she was still uneasy after last week's episode with the UPS driver, she didn't show it.

Cautioning himself not to get carried away with thoughts of what her skin felt like beneath his fingertips, of the lilac scent that emanated from her like a spring meadow, he glanced at the dish she carried.

She'd obviously been cooking. By now, that shouldn't have astonished him. Cynical-minded man that he was, it did.

He reached out, not sure whether to relieve her of the baby or the dish. He took the baby, the heaviest.

"Can I borrow the truck?" she asked, before he could even form a question of his own. "Just in case I need to use all four wheels."

He felt a smile pull at his mouth. She was so damned cute. "I hope you'd use all four regardless."

He looked down at the baby who was awake and round eyed, as though interested in the outdoor activity. His heart softened. She was a DeWitt now—there was a birth certificate naming him as father to prove it. All that he owned would be hers someday. He had an urge to show her around, then felt a little stupid at the thought. It wasn't as though a six-week-old baby could understand and appreciate his land.

"You know what I mean," Madison chided with a soft laugh. "I'd feel better in a four-wheel-drive vehicle in case of ice."

That got his attention right quick. "Where do you need to go? I'll drive you." His gaze kept straying to that covered dish. Whatever was in it smelled really good.

"No need for you to drive. You're busy. And I told Nancy and Letty I'd stop by the store. The church is organizing a bake sale and I promised to do my part."

"What's the occasion this time?" He felt odd asking her about the goings-on in his town. He also felt really good. Too good.

"Harvey Langford's boy got stepped on by a horse, and we're raising funds for the hospital bill." There was a river of compassion in both her voice and her china blue eyes.

"I know about his boy." He'd already written a check and mailed it anonymously to the hospital. Harvey had his pride. "You baked?"

She straightened to her full five-foot, three-inch height, looking for all the world like a puffed-up chinchilla who'd been insulted. Must have been all that fur outlining her face. He really ought to buy her a decent winter coat. And he didn't think she'd appreciate being compared to a chinchilla.

"Yes," she said, pride evident. "I baked. And it turned out great."

"You tasted it?"

"Not *this* one, silly. I made an extra cake for you and the men. That's the one I sampled. It's in the kitchen, so feel free to help yourselves. The keys?" She held out her hand.

He placed them in her palm without thought. "I'd feel better if I drove you."

"No you wouldn't. It would set you behind for the day, and you'd be a wreck."

"I'm never a wreck."

She reached out and patted his cheek, sending his blood pressure soaring. "Sorry. Didn't mean to insult your machismo."

He narrowed his eyes and fought a smile. The thing he realized about Madison Carlyle—DeWitt, he corrected himself—was that he truly *liked* her.

"What's the rope for?" she asked, eyeing the braided coil that he'd hitched over his shoulder when he'd taken the baby from her.

"Jared's due out to check on one of the cows. She's not eating and is getting weaker."

"Oh, the poor thing. What's wrong with her?"

"She's a gummer."

"A what?"

"Her teeth are worn away. I would have sold her during meat season, but she's a good breeder. I figured I could have Jared fit her with a set of false teeth and get a couple more productive seasons out of her. At this rate, though, she won't make it to spring."

"You provide dentistry for your cows?" Her astonished laughter tinkled on the cold wind as her breath blew silvery plumes of air.

He grinned. "Yeah. And my employees, too."

"What a guy."

He realized she'd hardly been out of the house since she'd been here, other than trips to church and their sleigh ride. "Want a quick tour of the barn, or do you have to get going?"

"I'd love one, if I wouldn't be keeping you from anything."

He hadn't realized he'd been holding his breath, waiting for her answer, hadn't realized how much her genuine interest would mean to him.

"I'm pretty much stuck until Simmons gets here." He opened the door of the truck. "Set the cake here on the seat."

She appeared just a bit reluctant. "Nobody will get it, will they?"

"I think it'll be safe enough—as long as Moe doesn't get a whiff. That man's got a sweet tooth that won't quit."

She placed the cake on the seat, having to shove aside all manner of tack and tools. "You wouldn't know it from looking at him. He's not overweight. Of course you guys are pretty physical."

Her appreciative gaze slid over him, making him sweat.

"I've warned you before about that particular look, sunshine."

She licked her lips, her eyes sparkling. "Obviously I don't pay a lot of heed to warnings."

Ah, but she did. She'd paid plenty of heed to the warning of danger to her child. It was the danger of intimacy between the two of them that didn't seem to have an impact.

On the one hand that made him really happy. On the other, it set his own caution sensors ringing. The closer they got, the harder it would be to let her go.

To watch her go.

She might be looking at him right now as her salvation, or, how had she put it? Ah, yes, her safe haven. But he had a sinking feeling it wouldn't last.

She'd been through hell—her child threatened, on the run while in labor, no less. Her proposal of a temporary marriage had been an act of desperation. Oh, sure, she was making the best of the circumstances, diving into the ranch with a zeal and determination that impressed him.

But he couldn't bring himself to trust what his eyes saw. Because in his heart he worried that, circumstances being what they were and all, she really wasn't certain of her wants. She couldn't be.

And that being the case, she was only playing at the life-style of being a rancher's wife.

For a while.

Before long—maybe a year, maybe two, perhaps only for the three months he'd agreed to—before long, she'd come to grips with what this was all about. She'd get tired of nothing fancier than Laurie's Café and limited menu, tired of traveling a hundred miles to a decent mall, of going forty miles just to see a show, tired of the small, close community that he valued so highly, tired of the frigid weather.

All it would take was an all-clear that the sperm donor's parents had no rights and she would be a free woman. Free to think straight, to walk out that door.

Free to take a piece of his heart with her when she left.

But right now she was looking to get a tour of his outbuildings, planning to take a covered dish to a bake sale for a good cause.

And right now was what he would think about. He'd worry about heartbreak later.

FOR THE REST OF THE DAY Brice couldn't stop thinking about Madison and the surprises she kept throwing at him. Baking cakes. Ironing creases in his jeans. Taking the pickup to town—alone. Interacting with the community and pitching in for the bake sales.

His ex-wife had never done any of those things, and she'd been here three years. Madison had only been here six weeks.

What next? he wondered.

He found out what next when he came in for supper. The house gleamed and smelled of furniture polish and fresh-baked bread. The baby gurgled happily in a bouncy seat he'd ordered along with the baby monitors. The floors and counters shone.

And now she was eyeing his dog.

"Jax, you need a bath."

Brice's brows shot up and he had a hard time keeping the silly grin off his face. He'd put in a full, hard day and was dead tired, yet one look at Madison and he felt renewed, energized, on top of the world.

Jax's ears perked up and he gave a canine expression of terror and pleading.

"Oh, show some courage, for pity's sake," she admonished the dog.

Brice figured he'd better intervene. After all, he and Jax had been an inseparable team until Madison and the baby had come along. Now the dog had taken to watching over the two females. Still, a guy had to stand up for his dog.

"Uh, don't go there, darlin'. Jax is like a cat when it comes to baths."

She whirled around, not realizing he was standing inside the doorway, listening to her conversation with the dog. "He smells," she complained.

Jax lowered his ears and whined.

"Aw, now you've insulted him."

Madison laughed. "I swear that dog understands me."

Jax barked.

"He does. Come on, boy. Might as well hit the showers with me." He snapped his fingers and Jax trotted to his side.

"You're going to shower *with* him?"

"You got a better idea?"

"Well, no. I've never bathed a dog before."

Because she'd probably never had pets, never got to stay in one place long enough to have them.

"This is the only way he'll agree to it. Besides, it's three below outside. He'd turn to an icicle."

She frowned. "I wouldn't suggest you take him outside."

"Then you were going to chance messing up your shiny floors?"

"Actually, I was only in the thinking stages. I hadn't gotten as far as the technicalities of how I'd accomplish the feat."

He grinned. "I'll help you out. Want to join us?"

He heard her breath catch, saw her cheeks darken with color. They were sharing a bed now, and their nights were filled with a passion he'd never known with any other woman. But, as though to stop any runaway emotions, to corral the hope, they'd only succumbed to passion in the bedroom. Now his fantasies were screaming to be set free.

But if he was going to turn his fantasies into reality, he wanted the time and concentration to fully appreciate, to store the memories.

"On second thought, never mind. When I take a shower with you, I don't want the dog between us."

IT HAD NEVER ANNOYED Brice before how people just walked into the house. But when Jared Simmons let himself in the back door without knocking, it bugged him. Especially when the vet immediately started flirting with Madison.

"Hey there, good-lookin'. Something sure smells good." Simmons pulled aside the sling that Madison wore across her chest and peeked at the baby.

Brice felt his blood pressure soar. He hadn't felt the urge to brawl in a long time.

Chair legs grated across tile as he stood. Both Madison and Jared gave him a questioning look.

"I'll take the baby." He lifted the sling over her head, carefully cradling Abbe. His fingers brushed the underside of Madison's breasts. It couldn't be helped. She jolted, her gaze snapping to his.

She stared at him for several heartbeats, then placed a gentle hand on his chest, soothing him when he didn't even realize he needed soothing.

"Thank you, Brice," she said softly. "Jared, would you like to stay for dinner?"

"Yeah. That'd be real nice. Provided DeWitt quits looking at me like he wants to punch my lights out."

"Oh, don't pay any attention to him," she said absently, pulling a pan of steaming biscuits out of the oven. "He scowls like that all the time."

"I do not," Brice objected. What had gotten into him? For crying out loud, Jared was his *friend*.

"Sit," Madison ordered.

Moe and the rest of the ranch hands came in, discarding outer gear and filling the kitchen with talk of cattle and downed fences and frozen troughs. And in between shop talk, they all hovered over Brice and the baby, cooing and clucking like a bunch of old women rather than crusty, hardworking cowboys.

Brice held the baby like a proud father, and the sight sent butterflies winging through Maddie's stomach. He was so good with Abbe. He was a man who should have a dozen kids. She remembered him telling her he *couldn't* have children, and wondered if there wasn't some test or new procedure that could help whatever plagued him. After all, modern medicine had come such a long way.

Abbe was a perfect example of that.

PROPPED IN BED, Brice watched Madison come out of the bathroom, the humidity of warm, lilac-scented steam fogging the windows. Normally he wouldn't be in bed so soon, would still be up doing paperwork. But Madison had his records so streamlined, there was little for him to do.

And though he knew it was wrong to get used to the intimacy of sharing a bed with her, he couldn't seem to work up the wherewithal to go back to sleeping in the guest room.

He felt like the luckiest man in the world, knowing that in just a few minutes she would ease into bed beside him, her talented fingers dancing over his skin.

The soft flannel of her gown clung to her moist body, outlining the curves he ached to touch, to possess, to hold on to forever.

But he couldn't think about forever, knew that wasn't in the cards.

He raised his arm when she walked toward him, making room for her against his side as she got into bed. Her skin smelled like a springtime meadow. But come spring, she'd likely be gone.

She shivered. "Even with the fire going, it's cold in here."

"Want me to close the window?"

She laid her head on his chest, snuggling. "No. I'm getting used to the scent of fresh air and the sounds of the animals that carry at night. Besides, you make a great furnace."

He tightened his arms around her, not wanting to turn out the light just yet. Her silky hair tickled his chin, and her breasts pressed softly against his side.

"Brice?"

"Hmm?"

"Can I ask you a personal question?"

"Mmm-hmm." He wondered what other little morsel of his life she'd unearthed in the pages of his check register.

"You mentioned once that you couldn't have children. What did you mean by that?"

His fingers paused in mid-stroke on her arm. He'd been prepared to defend or explain his life-style, not the state of his health. This was a touchy subject, one that dented his ego.

But Madison had shared so much of herself with him, he decided to return the favor. Besides, on the slim chance that she stayed beyond their three-month agreement, she needed to know up front that he couldn't be the one to provide her with more babies should she want them.

"Evidently I've got faulty sperm."

She rose up on an elbow, placed a palm over his heart, looked into his eyes. "Are you certain?"

He shrugged. "My ex and I weren't able to conceive. She was allergic to me." Saying it aloud still had the power to embarrass him, make him feel less a man. "And since she's remarried and expecting a child, I figure there's no question as to who was at fault."

"Perhaps it was just the two of you not being compatible."

He smiled, appreciating her giving him an out, letting him

save face. "We were incompatible in just about every way. Sharon hated it here, especially the winters."

She dropped a kiss on his jaw, then settled on top of him, aligning her body intimately with his, exerting just enough pressure to make him go from hard to steel in less than a second.

"The woman obviously doesn't have a speck of romance in her soul. Why, what female could resist the crackle of a fire and a sexy cowboy to keep her warm? Being forced indoors by the weather definitely has its merits."

He smoothed his hands down her back, rested his palms over her buttocks, pressed her against him, tortured himself. "Sunshine?"

"Hmm?" Her tongue swirled around his ear, her teeth nipped his lobe. And the friction of her body as she rubbed against him, the soft pillow of her breast against his chest, the provocative dip of her hips, was driving him mad.

"Can we not talk about my ex anymore?" Rather than wait for an answer, he rolled her beneath him, slipped her gown over her head and tossed it on the floor. "I've got plans for that sexy body of yours, and there's only room for the two of us in this bed."

"Oh, I do like it when you come up with plans."

He chuckled, surprised. With Madison, he'd found that lovemaking didn't always have to be serious. There was room to laugh, to play.

"You smell good." He skimmed the outer curve of her breast with his lips and tongue.

"Mmm. Baby talc." Her breath hitched as his fingers stroked her, teased, then slipped inside.

"And lilacs. It's an erotic combination."

That wasn't the only erotic combination. His clever fingers and lips took her desire from hot to flash point in a split second. She placed her hand over his, tilted her hips off the bed, struggling to draw a breath.

Dear heaven, it got better every time. And though she longed to savor the exquisite touch of this man, her husband, she couldn't wait. Desperation was like a living, breathing entity inside her.

"Now, Brice. I want you inside me."

She saw a vein pulse at his temple, knew it was taking everything he possessed to keep a rein on his control. She wanted him to lose that control, to not think, to only feel.

To feel her love.

She reached for him, wrapped her fingers around him, urged him, guided him.

And when he entered her, his movements were as desperate as hers, as though he were trying to pack a lifetime of memories into just a few short hours.

And, wanting those memories, that lifetime—yet so afraid it might not be—she matched his desperation, moving with him, holding him, letting her body speak the words she wasn't free to say aloud.

I love you.

Pleasure spiraled, a white-hot flash of heat that throbbed clear to her soul, snatched her breath, blanked her mind of all else. Just sensation…shattering, exquisite sensation.

It was almost too much. For a minute she felt as though she were about to black out, to faint from the pure unadulterated pleasure. Colors exploded behind her eyelids, vibrant and erotic, as she came apart, inch by glorious inch.

For what seemed like hours, he held her close, their breathing labored. She felt sluggish—as though she'd been pleasantly drugged—yet empowered.

She was smart enough to know that what they shared in this bed was rare; that their explosive sexual compatibility wasn't something that happened often or on a regular basis.

When she was with Brice, it was as if they were part of each other, so in sync. At least in bed.

He eased off her, gathered her close. "Still cold?"

She smiled, even though every muscle in her body had turned to mush. "Now that's a provocative question. Ask me again in ten minutes, and I'll be up for the challenge."

He kissed her temple. "I swear you'll wear me out."

"I doubt it." She ran a hand over his biceps, loving the rock-hard feel of him beneath her palm, the strength. These well-defined muscles hadn't come from a pricey gym. They'd been honed from lifting fifty-pound saddles, roping calves and hefting bales of hay and feed for animals. Ranching was physical work, and Brice DeWitt was a very physical man.

"You look like a pretty strong guy to me. Besides, I seem to recall a certain fantasy you had that involved those woollies." Or had that been her fantasy?

His laugh was muffled against her hair. "You are a shameless woman."

Her heart pounded at the image of him, naked except for fleece-covered chaps tied high on his thighs. She closed her eyes and groaned, pressing against him, feeling desire build all over again. What in the world had gotten into her. She wasn't normally such a sexually obsessed woman.

"I do like your cowboy outfits. A bit different from what I'd seen in the Dallas honky-tonks, though."

"Those guys are probably a bunch of corporate cowboys who've never even been on a horse."

"You may be right. Their boots were awfully shiny." She ran her bare foot up his calf. "How come you don't wear spurs on your boots? Isn't that supposed to be standard issue?"

"Not on my ranch. I don't believe in them, and I don't allow the men who work for me to wear them, either. My cow ponies are well trained to stop and turn in an instant. If a cowhand can't get the horse to mind, he's no horseman and doesn't belong on the Flying D."

He was really fierce about the subject, and it gave Maddie just that much more insight into this special man. He had a tough hide, but inside was a gentle streak that was unmistakable—for people as well as his animals.

The baby monitor on the nightstand crackled as Abbe shifted in her crib and let out a soft cry.

Maddie and Brice froze, afraid if they made a move or a

noise it would wake the baby all the way. Ridiculous, since their daughter was clear in the other room.

The minute Maddie realized she'd thought of Abbe as *their* daughter, something bittersweet shifted inside her.

It was a hope, a dream really, that she didn't dare dwell on. Because life had a way of throwing curve balls when least expected. And the possibility that her tiny baby could be taken from her didn't even bear thinking about.

She'd go underground before she'd let that happen.

And if it came to that, it would mean leaving Brice. Oh, dear God, the choice would tear her in two.

Desperation had her arms tightening around his chest as a strange sadness built inside her, a premonition of dark shadows lurking.

Brice felt her tension and soothed with a palm at her back. "I think she's okay. Sounds like she's going back to sleep. Want me to go check on her, anyway?"

Maddie snuggled into the protective circle of his arms, trying to banish the gloom of her thoughts, her waking nightmare.

"No. I can't pick her up every time she fusses." But she wanted to. She wanted to hold her baby daughter, protect her and never let go.

Just like she never wanted to let go of Brice.

BRICE LOOKED UP at the clear blue sky dotted with puffy white clouds. So far they'd had a really mild winter, not nearly the snowfall that they normally got.

It was early March, and the three-month deadline for reassessing his and Madison's marriage was approaching way too fast. She seemed happy here, blending in with the men and the people of the community, never complaining about the cold or the chores, the long hours he spent outdoors or the lack of a social life.

Maybe the three-month date would just come and go, slip by like a silent thief without crossing his threshold. Perhaps if they just ignored it, one day would segue into the next until they both woke up some morning and realized they'd actually grown old together.

Hell, he was being fanciful and melancholy. And that wasn't like him. Damn it, he had work to do. He tugged at the brim of his hat, dusted flecks of hay off his shoulder. He was jumpy today and couldn't put his finger on the reason.

Coming out of the barn, he pinpointed the cause.

A luxury Cadillac turned in off the highway, looking so out of place he stood and stared.

Then it hit him, the suspicion…the realization.

Madison's ticking time bomb had just exploded.

Chapter Thirteen

Brice had an overpowering urge to run, to race against the seconds slipping away, to grab Madison and Abbe and hide, shield them.

But it was too late. The Cadillac had already stopped by the front porch, and a well-dressed man and woman got out of the car. Would Madison refuse to open the door like she had when Mike Collier had shown up?

Look out the window, sunshine. Hide.

He was a step away from the porch, behind the older couple.

"Can I help you folks with something?"

Before he could even get the sentence all the way out, the front door opened.

"Brice, do you know where the—" Madison's words broke off. Obviously she hadn't seen the car, was stunned that strangers were on the porch. Her expression went from inquisitive, to dawning surprise, to panic in the space of a heartbeat. Clearly, she'd just realized she'd let down her guard too soon. And look at the consequences—assuming, of course, that these people were who he thought they were.

He moved past the older couple to Madison's side, slipped an arm around her waist, gathered her close. Abbe, nearly three months old now, was dressed in a pink blanket sleeper with a frilly bib tied around her sweet neck. She'd started drooling a lot lately. Plus she liked to smile when she was supposed to be drinking a bottle, causing smelly formula to run down her pudgy cheeks and into the folds of her neck, then soaking the front of her outfit.

His fingers tightened at Madison's waist. By God, nobody was going to mess with his family, nobody else was going to capture the precious moments of this baby's toothless smile, the way her eyes lit up and her legs churned and kicked. Nobody but him and Madison.

"My name's Winslow Covington, and this is my wife, Lila."

Out of courtesy, Brice accepted the man's outstretched hand, making a quick visual assessment of the people who'd threatened Madison with a custody battle.

They looked in their early fifties—fit, curious, stubborn. Lila's full-length mink coat and Winslow's cashmere overcoat spoke of wealth, but that didn't bother Brice. He was wealthy in his own right, a match for these folks. He just didn't flaunt his bank account through his wardrobe and classy vehicles.

"Brice DeWitt." He dropped Winslow's hand, noticing that the Covingtons' avid attention was on the baby Madison held in her arms. "And this is my wife and daughter." Their name omission was deliberate. He wanted to know the Covingtons' intent before he went any further.

"You had a little girl," Lila whispered, her jewelry-adorned hands trembling as she clutched the lapel of her mink coat.

Maddie shifted Abbe in her arms, her shoulders squaring. "Yes. I have a daughter."

"We've spent a fair amount of time and money searching for you, Ms. Carlyle."

"DeWitt," Brice corrected. "And out of curiosity, why would you want to search for my wife?"

"Didn't she tell you? That baby she conceived is our grand-child—though we'd been told it was a boy."

Brice's eyes narrowed, and his gut tightened. How dare they think any less of the baby because of her sex. He tugged the brim of his hat, shot this snooty rich man a look that didn't take a genius to figure out.

"Funny, you're no kin to me, so I don't see how you can claim you're my daughter's grandparents." His voice was quiet, yet it rang like a shout in the still, morning air. "And I gotta tell you, the fact that you'd even come here saying something like that puts me in a mind to get the shotgun, maybe do a little target practice with that fancy Caddie."

Winslow backed up a step. Lila gasped, her kohl-lined eyes going wide.

Madison stunned all of them by smothering a nervous laugh. "Brice, stop it. Listen, it's cold out here, and the baby's not dressed for an outdoor chat." She looked up at him. "Would you mind if the Covingtons came inside?"

When he glanced down at her, the brim of his hat touched her forehead, creating a shadow over the three of them. "Actually, I think I do mind. Kinda like inviting the coyote into the barn, don't you think?"

"Maybe so. But I need to get this settled. I'm tired of looking over my shoulder." She glanced at the Covingtons, her expression determined, her shoulders squared with that bravado he so admired about her. "I'm willing to hear you out, but that's it. You don't have any claim whatsoever on my daughter."

Brice hoped to God Madison's words were correct. Coward that he was, he'd never gotten around to calling his attorney. He'd been afraid of the answer he'd get.

"Humph," Winslow muttered. "Think you can hold your own against us in a court of law? Could get expensive. Do you have the financial resources to play with the big boys?"

"*I* do," Brice said, the steel in his voice cracking like a bullwhip even though he never raised his tone, kept it conversational, friendly even. "Now, I'd be much obliged if you'd get off my property before I forget I'm a civilized man and knock those expensive caps down your throat."

He gave the older man points for standing his ground. Winslow's chest puffed out, and he took a tentative step forward.

Brice dropped his arm from around Madison, matched Covington's stance, taunted him even. God he wanted a fight, a release of these raw emotions that were eating away at him, the emotions he'd been battling since the day Madison and Abbe had entered his life, worked their way into his heart.

He cocked a brow in invitation, his teeth bared in a smile that would have had his cowhands ducking for cover. "You're thinking about it, hmm? Well come on, then. Just step off the porch, away from the ladies."

Lila drew in a breath and smacked her husband in the chest, even though it had been Brice who'd issued the challenge. "Winslow! Stop this insanity. I knew you'd make a mess of this!" Tears filled her eyes.

Madison stepped in front of Brice, gave him an incredulous look. "What in the name of peace has gotten into you?"

"I'm not feeling the least peaceable right now, sunshine."

"Well...well, just calm down. I'll not have anybody brawling on the front porch."

He acquiesced with a slight nod of his head, but it was evident that he was still a tiny bubble away from a rolling boil. "If you have anything further to say to my wife, you can do it through our attorneys."

"Please," Lila Covington whispered, the single word so stark, so raw, that Maddie nearly reached out to comfort her.

Now where had that uncharacteristic urge come from? she wondered. She wasn't normally a woman given to shows of compassion and...and well, she was surprised at herself. This Wyoming friendliness must be rubbing off on her.

Lila folded her hands in what could have been a gesture of prayer or restraint, as though she ached to touch the baby but feared the reprisals of the uninvited act.

And Maddie probably wouldn't have let either one of these people touch Abbe, regardless of Lila's seemingly genuine tears.

She pulled the blanket up over Abbe's head, since it appeared they were destined to entertain from the open doorway on the porch. At least the warmth of the fire was at her back, though if she didn't shut the door soon, the house was going to be as cold as the outdoors.

Winslow looked down at his wife. "Darrell told us the child was a boy. Clearly things have changed now."

Brice closed his hand into a fist, emotions flying at him so fast he couldn't field them. If Madison hadn't chosen that precise moment to hook her finger through one of his belt loops and tug, he would have taken a poke at the guy, regardless of her admonitions of brawling on the porch and the man being twenty years his senior.

"So," Brice said, so livid he could hardly get the words out, "since the baby's a girl you're not so sure you're willing to fight the fight, huh?" Damn it, he felt like these people were rejecting this precious baby. His baby. And he wouldn't stand for it. Never mind that their rejection was just what Madison wanted. It was the principle of the matter. His daughter's honor. "I'd like to hit you."

Winslow raised his gaze from his wife's tear-streaked face. "Please don't, young man. I can be a pompous ass, and Lila tells me I don't have a bit of tact." He paused, pressed his thumb and finger to his eyes, then squeezed the bridge of his nose. "We lost our son. It's made us a little crazy. I only wanted to help my wife." He swallowed hard. "And myself—we had to know…"

Dear God, they'd been bluffing. Out of grief.

Madison stepped forward then, put her hand on Lila's mink-covered arm. "Please come in out of the cold," she said gently, then gave Brice a defiant look that fairly dared him to try and overrule her.

They went inside, sat down. No one bothered to remove their coats as it was chilly in the room. Maddie had the warmth of her daughter to ward off the cold.

Brice put another log on the fire, then came to sit by Maddie, presenting a united front. Her heart swelled, and she fell a little more in love with him, if that were possible.

"Mr. Covington, you mentioned the name Darrell—"

"The private investigator we hired. He came out with the United Parcel man, told us you matched the picture we'd provided. The child appeared the right age for the term of your pregnancy."

"And what gave you the impression I'd had a boy?"

"Darrell said the child was wrapped in a blue blanket."

Maddie remembered the day Ken had shown up with a trainee. And she remembered Brice coming out on the porch, with Abbe swaddled in a blue blanket, the first one he'd snatched after changing her diapers.

Curious, though, that this Darrell person hadn't bothered to ask Ken about Abbe. "How did he find me?"

"I'm afraid I didn't ask that question. I was merely interested in the bottom line, the outcome."

"To take away my baby?"

Lila had the grace to look ashamed, and Maddie realized she was the one to appeal to—mother to mother.

"Mrs. Covington, I'm sorry for the loss of your son. I didn't know him, but I'm sure he was a fine young man and you loved him very much. Can't you see, though, that your threats put me in the same position? Of losing *my* child?"

"I didn't think. When I found record of Stephen donating sperm, all I could focus on was that a part of him would still live on, and that if I could get that piece back, his baby, it would ease the loss of not having Stephen with us anymore."

"Stephen was the last of our blood," Winslow added. "Our only hope to carry on the family name."

"You don't need a DNA match to carry on a name," Brice said quietly.

Maddie looked at him. Lord he was a special man. She knew he loved Abbe and that he would always consider her a DeWitt.

And because of his generosity, she could be generous, too. Lila and Winslow Covington were racked with grief, and they'd jumped on any means to assuage their pain. The product of their son's donated sperm could give them peace.

She rose with Abbe in her arms. "Would you like to hold her?"

The look on Lila's face was so full of hope and joy it nearly brought Maddie to tears.

"Oh, may I?"

Carefully she transferred the baby to Lila's arms. Winslow leaned in close, his features going soft as he thumbed the moisture from beneath his wife's eyes, then rested his gaze on Abbe.

"What did you name her?" Lila asked.

"Abigail. We call her Abbe."

Lila smiled, stroked a gentle finger over Abbe's downy soft cheek, smoothed the tiny, paper-thin fingernails. "What a beautiful name. What a beautiful little girl." She looked up at Maddie. "I'm so sorry for the way we frightened you. We had no right to make horrible threats. I know you've given up your home and your business. We'd like to make it up to you." She shot her husband a stern look. "Wouldn't we, Winslow?"

"Of course, dear."

Maddie shook her head. "There's no need. My daughter is a gift more priceless than any amount of money."

Abbe started to fuss, perhaps picking up on the thick emotions in the room, the new set of arms holding her. Lila stood and gently placed the baby back in Madison's arms, her hand lingering for a moment longer, her gaze clinging, searching for that visual likeness—a tie to her son.

And being a mother, understanding the profound love, unable to even think of the horror and pain of what it would be like to lose a child, Madison's heart ached for Lila and Winslow Covington.

"I can't replace your son, but I don't want to keep your granddaughter from you. If you're interested in being part-time grandparents, it would be wonderful for Abbe to get to know you."

"Oh, Madison. You can't know how those words make me

feel. We would love to be part of her life, as much or as little as you'll allow. And...well," Lila lowered her voice, glanced to where Brice stood stiffly by the sofa, then looked back at Maddie. "I'm so glad to know that you're settled, that you've found someone who loves both you and the baby." She hesitated, her brows drawing together. "You *are* settled, aren't you? Everything is okay between you and your husband?"

Now this was the sticky part. "Yes," Maddie admitted. But for how long? Now that the threat was over, would he still welcome her to stay? And as what? A housekeeper who just happens to sleep with him.

Maddie wanted more. She wanted love.

Lila must have picked up on Maddie's disquiet because the look in her eyes was woman-to-woman, the sort of look that speaks louder than words.

"We won't push. But if you're ever in need, we have an obscenely large home on the outskirts of Dallas. You and Abbe would want for nothing. And, well...I don't want to overstep here, but I'm trying to let you know that you're always welcome." She pressed a card with their phone number in Maddie's hand.

"Thank you." The card burned in her hand and she glanced at Brice, wondering if he'd overheard the invitation. Wondering if he'd care. Wondering if he'd welcome the chance to get rid of her. Other than the slight frown, she couldn't tell what he was thinking.

She looked back at Lila and said very softly, "I'm going to try really hard to make a go of it here."

Lila nodded. "You'll be a fine mother to our granddaughter."

With a final lingering look, the Covingtons went down the porch steps arm in arm and got into their Cadillac.

When Maddie turned, Brice was already pulling on his gloves. He was wearing a new pair of jeans—she knew that because the hem was stacked on his boots, nearly dragging the ground around his boot heel. He didn't have on his chaps today, just body-hugging denim, a wide belt with a silver buckle, a heavy, plaid flannel shirt and the requisite bandanna tied around his neck.

And of course his hat.

"You should wear a white hat," she blurted.

He stepped closer to her, tilted his head, the intense look in his dark blue eyes making her shiver. "Why?"

"Because you're one of the good guys."

"Don't be too sure of that. I wanted to take Covington apart with my bare hands."

"I know. And that makes you a good guy."

"Brawling on the porch?"

"No. Protecting. Caring." She searched his gaze, willed him to give her an indication that he felt more, that he wanted her to stay, that things wouldn't change now that the Covingtons were no longer a threat.

Kiss me, she wanted to say. *Hold me.*

But she didn't utter either one of those pleas. She wouldn't beg, had learned at an early age never to show that vulnerability. A kid who asked for too much was invariably sent away. And though she was no longer a child, the lesson was indelibly burned in her mind.

"Out here that's standard. We protect our own." Brice saw her wince, knew she'd expected more from him, something more personal, words that didn't lump her and the baby in the same category as a distant neighbor or one of his cows.

But he couldn't give her those words, couldn't give her those assurances. Because if he did, he might sway her thinking. There was nothing keeping her here now. And he'd heard Lila Covington offering her a place to live.

A fancy city place, with city conveniences and city people to interact with. A lot more attractive than just the few families that made up their small community here, or the bitter winters and scorching summers.

It was only a matter of time before Madison realized that,

only a matter of time before she left. And he didn't know how to stop her. So he pulled back, insulating himself.

"I better get back to work."

"You're not wearing a coat."

"I've been mucking stalls and feeding stock. A coat just gets in my way." He wanted to reach out and touch her instead of having a ridiculous conversation about his apparel. To prevent himself from doing just that, he turned and headed for the door. Before he'd made it outside, though, the two-way base-unit radio crackled with static. Changing directions, he went into his office.

"This here's Sully calling the Flying D. Come on back to me, over."

Brice lifted the mike and pressed the transmit button. "Brice, here, Sully. What's up."

"Got us a hungry wolf attacking the cattle. Wily sucker. And sure as we go off tracking him, a storm'll blow in and we'll spill the herd. I figure we could use a couple more bodies to cover so we can scout him out."

There were three men at the line camp, and it would take two of them to keep the cows from wandering—or spilling—if a storm came up. The animals would move right along with the wind if the cowhands didn't keep them corralled. And it wasn't wise to send only one man out tracking a wolf.

"I'll bring Dan and Randy and be up there by nightfall."

"Roger, boss. We'll sit tight till we hear from you. You might check with the neighbors, too, see if any of their cattle are turning up dead. If he's killing with any sort of pattern, maybe we can get a better fix on his location."

"I'll do that." Brice replaced the mike. He could have just sent Dan and Randy, but this was the perfect excuse to get away from the ranch, to have some breathing room, to steel himself for the loneliness of when Madison left.

"Do you often have trouble with wolves getting your cows?" Madison asked.

Brice turned, not realizing she'd followed him into the office.

She motioned toward the two-way radio on the desk. "I heard your conversation with Sully."

"There's always the danger—even more so in the winter when it's harder for them to come by food."

"Is it dangerous? For you to go looking for the wolf, I mean."

"Not when I'm the one holding the rifle."

Moe wandered into the office, clutching his battered hat in his hand. "What's the holdup? Thought you was givin' the bulls a snack, and when I didn't see hide nor hair of ya, I 'bout decided some critter'd had *you* for a snack."

"Naw. I'm in one piece." Bodily. He couldn't say as much for his heart. "We've lost a few head of beef to the wolves, though."

"Best we get to trackin' then."

Madison whirled into action. "You'll need hot coffee, some food supplies. How long will you be gone?"

"A couple days."

"I'll put some things together for you."

"There's a cabin out where we're going. And it's fully stocked."

"Then I'll at least send you with a thermos of coffee. And some of my bread."

Brice opened his mouth to tell her not to bother, but she'd already bustled out of the room. And why shouldn't she bother? She was still his housekeeper.

And his wife.

Damn it. He ran a hand over the back of his neck, feeling weary, not wanting to leave, yet desperate to get away. He was a mess. He couldn't even make up his mind or get his thoughts to march in a straight line.

"Don't know why yer kickin' up a ruckus over coffee and carrot bread. It'll taste mighty fine after that cold ride. Be a treat for Sully and Luke."

"I guess I'm not used to somebody fussing."

"Humph." Moe's shrewd gaze fastened onto Brice, making him squirm. "Didn't think it was fussin' when Lavina cooked up vittles to go."

The older man saw more than Brice wanted him to. "You're gnawing at a carcass that's been picked clean, Bertelli. As an employer, I'm worried about Madison being here at the ranch on her own."

"An employer? She's yer *wife,* boy, or did ya forget? And what the Sam Hill does stayin' by herself have to do with fixin' a jug of coffee?"

"She's only my temporary wife."

"Don't act temporary to me. 'Specially seein' as how you're sharin' that bedroom with her."

The censure in Moe's voice was unmistakable, and Brice couldn't evade or excuse. He felt like a horse thief who'd stolen something that wasn't his to begin with.

He'd stolen moments with Madison.

But he wasn't going to be dressed down in his own house, no matter how much he respected Moe Bertelli.

"*I'm* not the one who'll leave. I'm part of this land. And you ought to know better than I do that women don't stay."

"Miss Maddie's different. That girl's got real deep feelings in her heart."

"What makes you so sure? Seems to me you thought the same thing about Sharon. She left. And how'd you feel about my mother? You knew her better than me. You saw how she treated Dad. How she just left."

"You can't be judging everybody by the same dang fence post."

"I'm being realistic. She comes from the city. Just like my mother did. Just like Sharon did. If she'd grown up on a sheep ranch in Australia or something, I might feel different. But she didn't. And I don't."

With each word he said, Moe's expression got darker. "Confound it, boy. Tryin' to get through that thick skull of yours is enough to make a preacher cuss."

Brice sighed, feeling weary. "I'm trying to protect my heart," he admitted before he could stop himself.

"Maybe yer tryin' too hard, and it don't need protectin'."

"Maybe. Maybe not." He looked at his watch. "I've gotta go meet up with Sully before dark."

"Then we best get to movin'."

"Not we. I want you to stay here."

Moe puffed out his chest. "Don't think I'm too old to take you down a peg or two, boy. I'll not stand for you treatin' me with kid gloves."

"I'm not." And he truly meant it. Usually he had to be fairly inventive in his excuses to get Moe to stay at the ranch. This time, there was no subterfuge. "I need someone to stay with Madison and the baby. She's not used to this life. If the power goes out, she wouldn't know how to fire up the generator, and chances are she's never been in a blizzard before. I couldn't concentrate if I was worried about her and the baby being here alone in bad weather conditions."

"Nobody said we was in for a blizzard," Moe pointed out cagily. "I reckon that fence around your heart ain't so sturdy after all. And that bein' the case, I'd be right proud to stay here and watch over your family."

Brice's gut clenched, and he didn't trust himself to speak.

Your family.

God Almighty, he'd give anything if that were so.

Chapter Fourteen

He'd been gone nearly a week, stuck at the line camp because of a storm. It had been a miserable five days of trying to keep the herd together and hay on the ground.

They hadn't seen any more signs of the wolf that had been stalking his cattle, and Brice knew he needed to get back to the ranch, yet a heavy reluctance assailed him. Would Madison still be there? Or had she decided to head back to the city, to take the Covingtons up on their offer? Although he'd checked in with Moe a couple of times, he hadn't been able to bring himself to ask about her.

He was steeling himself for the emptiness, the pain.

Damn it, he'd sworn he wouldn't let his heart get involved, wouldn't go through that kind of despair again.

And he'd failed miserably.

He looked around him, noticing the elk tracks in the snow. He'd left before Dan and Randy, needing to be alone with his thoughts, to mask his emotions before he rode into the ranch. The men were probably only about ten minutes behind him.

A different set of tracks caught his eye. Wolf tracks.

He pulled his rifle out of the scabbard and gave Samson a gentle nudge, following the trail that led along the base of the mountains. To his left was steep terrain dotted with lodgepole pines, their evergreen needles frosted with snow. To the right was vast, open prairie that gave way to gently rolling hills and deep gulches. In the distance he could see a ribbon of asphalt, the main highway leading into town that Leonard must have plowed. All the neighbors pitched in to keep the roads cleared, but Leonard was the most diligent.

The animal tracks made a sudden zigzag, then veered to the right. "Come on, Samson. Let's see what this sucker's up to."

He tugged at the brim of his hat and hunched his shoulders beneath his coat. The smell of pine and clean air mixed with the scents of leather and horse. Familiar smells, peaceful, but it was damned cold out here.

The wolf tracks disappeared over the top of a rise, and Brice dismounted, gripping his rifle in a gloved hand. The snow was deeper here, but he trudged through, determined to catch sight of that wolf.

He realized his mistake at the last minute. This wasn't the crest of a hill. It was a snowdrift at the edge of a narrow gully.

He knew better.

The rock beneath his boot heel gave out and it was too late to back away to safety. The ground shifted, giving beneath his weight. The force of his body sliding downward dislodged the snow, creating a small avalanche.

The rifle flew from his hand, and he tumbled. His shoulder banged against unforgiving rock. His hat went sailing. His boots met him, then vanished from sight as he somersaulted down the steep incline.

Time moved in slow motion—the adage about a person's life flashing before their eyes was proved to him in spades. The main part of his life he saw was the part with Madison. And he was aware of the pain of never seeing her and the baby again.

With her name on his lips, pain lanced through his skull, sharp and debilitating as his head cracked against blunt, unforgiving land. Then there was only darkness.

MADISON WAS WORRIED. A week had passed since Brice had gone to the line camp. A blinding snowstorm had blown a blanket of white over everything, piling drifts clear up to the windows.

Having never seen weather like this, Maddie had been intrigued—until she'd realized that the nasty storms were keeping Brice from coming home.

She'd been monitoring the two-way radio, thrilled to just listen to the sound of his voice. Even though he hadn't contacted her directly, she'd followed his communications with his men. Out on the range, each man wore a walkie-talkie unit and kept in close touch with one another, working as a team.

And according to those conversations, the men were on their way home. They hadn't yet tracked down the wolf, but she knew they were still searching, fanning in a sweep that would eventually end back here at the ranch.

Static crackled again over the radio. This was the third time Dan, Randy and Mike had checked in.

But Brice wasn't responding. She could hear the edge in Dan's voice, and her stomach fluttered in alarm.

Something was terribly wrong.

"Moe!" Her shout startled Abbe who whimpered for a second, then settled as though realizing this wasn't a good time to raise a fuss.

Moe came charging into the room, lickety-split. "What?"

"Something's wrong. Brice isn't answering his radio."

Moe frowned and keyed the mike. "This here's base. Brice? You out there, son? Come in."

Silence.

Maddie counted the seconds, *one thousand and one, one thousand and two,* as though judging the distance of a lightning strike.

The radio crackled. She hovered closer, crowding Moe.

Dan's voice, sounding tinny and concerned, came over the radio. "The boss hasn't answered for fifteen minutes. He went off on his own, but we've lost his tracks. The drifts are so high it's hard to keep our bearings. We can't see the fence tops."

"Why do they want to see the fences?" Maddie asked.

"For directions," Moe said. "It'll guide 'em home when the visibility's bad." He keyed the mike again. "Brice? Answer me, you son of a gun."

Radio silence.

"Damn." Randy's voice this time. "Wish somebody had a plane. It's damn cold out here, and we're going in circles. A recon by air would be best. You want to contact Search and Rescue, Moe?"

"Brice has a plane," Maddie said, gripping Moe's shirt-sleeve.

He looked at her, compassion in his hazel eyes. He was worried and trying hard to hide it. "Yeah, but we ain't got no pilot."

"I'm a pilot."

His gray brows lifted, then he shook his head. "Brice would pitch a fit if I let you go tearing off in his Cessna."

"I'd welcome him throwing a fit—as long as he's here. Safe."

"Let's give it a few minutes. Could be he's behind a hill and the radio's actin' up."

Her heart pounded louder than the ticking of the old grand-father clock that stood in the corner. Nausea welled but she battled it back, placing her palm low on her stomach and breath-ing deep. A few days ago, Nancy Adams had confirmed what Maddie had suspected for a couple of weeks now. There was another small life counting on Brice to come home.

Certain she would scream if she had to endure one more second of inactivity, she held out her hand for the mike.

"We can't leave him out there, Moe. He's had plenty of time to get back in radio range. Something's wrong. I feel it. You know I'm his best chance right now."

He hesitated, studying her with a shrewdness that took her aback, then nodded and passed her the mike.

She took a deep breath, praying she was up to the task she'd just assigned herself. Praying they'd find Brice before the ele-ments got to him first.

"Okay, you guys. This is Maddie. Which one of you is the closest to the ranch?"

The three men gave their approximate positions.

"I'm five minutes from you," Mike Collier said. He was the new hired hand that Maddie had been so suspicious of. At least now she knew he wasn't a spy.

"Then meet me at the hangar."

"Come again?" Dan this time, sounding confused.

"The airstrip. I'm taking Brice's plane up and I need the runway plowed. I'll coordinate once I get in the air." From the window she could see Mike Collier galloping toward the barn, leading another horse by a rope.

She whirled toward Moe. "That's not Brice's horse, is it?" Her words came out in a breathy rush as adrenaline pumped through her.

Moe glanced out the window. "No. Just a pack horse."

She let out a relieved breath, replaced the radio mike, then pressed a lingering kiss to her baby daughter's forehead.

"Can you handle Abbe while I'm gone?"

"'Course I can," Moe said gruffly. "Just give me that new-fangled sling thing, and I'll harness her right in here." Maddie adjusted the sling around his neck then placed Abbe in it, resting against his chest. "Just don't go rootin' around for something that ain't there, sweet pea."

Maddie reached out, gripped Moe's gnarled hand. He gave a squeeze. "Go on and get. I'll round up the neighbors to help in the search. You jest be careful, hear?"

"I will. Thanks, Moe." She kissed his cheek, then grabbed her coat and gloves and sprinted outside. The keys were already in the truck, and she barely gave the engine time to warm up before she was headed toward the airstrip, the tires spinning and slipping. Afraid she'd wreck the pickup before she even got to the hangar, she made herself ease up on the gas.

The snow wasn't falling, thank God. She looked up through the windshield to the sky. Clouds at about a thousand feet and getting lower, a bit unstable, but do-able. If she stayed low, she should be able to fly under them.

Mike Collier had already opened the huge metal door of the hangar and was now making a pass over the airstrip with the plow truck.

Hands sweating, nerves screaming, she inspected the single-engine, fixed-wing tail dragger. She'd flown one before, and though her confidence was shaky, at least she didn't have to worry that the aircraft wasn't mechanically sound. Brice kept all of his equipment in top-notch condition. She knew that from the regular ledger entries under Maintenance and Repair.

Still, it had been a while since she'd flown, and she was apprehensive. But she didn't have a choice. Brice needed her. And she would be there for him. He was a man who took care of everyone else, yet when he was in need, the women in his life had let him down.

That was going to change. She wouldn't let him down like the others had.

Determination pushing past the fear, she kicked the shims away from the front of the tires, glancing up as Mike came into the cavernous hangar.

"Can you help me push it out?"

Silently he gripped the strut under the wing and gave a shove. Madison pushed from her side and the Cessna rolled forward, clearing the building.

The air was so cold her cheeks stung, but nerves made her sweat beneath the bulky sweater and thermal shirt. In her rush, she'd left her coat lying on the front seat of the truck.

The wind wasn't blowing much which was a plus. She was damned rusty at flying and she didn't need heavy gusts to battle—especially in a plane that was trickier than most on takeoffs and landings.

"Good luck," Mike said. "I'll run another pass over the runway, make sure it's clear."

"Thanks." After a quick preflight inspection, she climbed into the cockpit, folded herself into the tight quarters and buckled her harness. She wanted to hurry, but knew that was folly. She checked gauges, plugged in the radio headset, then started the single engine, her heart pumping a mile a minute as the motor caught on the first revolution. Leaning forward, she flipped dials on the radio.

"Moe? Do you read?" Nerves made her voice all breathy and trembly, as though she'd just finished a marathon run.

"Yep. I'm here, missy. You figure out how to get that tin can goin'?"

"I'm heading for the runway now." Such as it was. It was little more than an eight-hundred-foot strip of asphalt out in the middle of nowhere. Well, not nowhere. Brice's ranch. Her home.

"You watch them clouds, Miss Maddie. If it looks to be blowin' up another storm, you head back in, hear me?"

"I hear you, Moe."

"I mean it. Ain't no use to the little one if both you and Brice are lost."

She didn't respond. She had no intention of getting lost—or of coming back without Brice.

The Cessna's engine revved in time with her pulse, vibrating through her chest. Her palms were slick inside her leather gloves.

"Here goes." She checked the flaps and pulled the throttle. Slushy mounds of snow, piled on the sides of the asphalt, whizzed by faster and faster as the plane gained momentum. At the end of the strip, Mike Collier stood on the running board of the snowplow, watching, then whipped off his hat and waved it as though offering encouragement—or prayers.

She handled the aircraft with an ease and confidence that surprised her, given the fact that she hadn't been in a cockpit for a while. Her flight instructors had always complimented her on her technique, though, the innate way she felt each shimmy and shift of a plane, the way she flew by instinct.

She pulled back on the yoke. The plane's nose angled up and the tail lifted off the ground. She loved this feeling of power, the gentle soar into the sky, the tickle in her midsection as though her stomach hadn't quite caught up with the airspeed.

And now that she was airborne, she needed to get her bearings.

She keyed the radio. "Guys, check in."

"Dan here. I'm in the truck with Mike."

"Randy here. I'm on horseback just coming up on Little Bear Creek."

Maddie frowned. "I'm not familiar with that area, Randy. What are the coordinates with regard to the ranch?"

"Sorry, Miss Maddie…that'd put me about five miles south of the barn."

She nodded to herself, then jumped when another voice came over the radio.

"This here's Harvey Langford. Me and three of the boys are heading west from our spread. Two of us are on horseback, and the other two are in the 'cowboy Cadillac.'"

The what? Madison wondered. Before she could ask for clarification, another of her neighbors checked in.

"Jack Springer, Miz DeWitt. Langford's talking about the pickup, in case you were wondering. I'm headed from the east. There's two of us on snowmobiles. Letty's closed up the store in town and is headed out to your place. No telling who she's got with her."

"I heard that, Jack Springer." Letty's voice now. "You just pay attention to what you're doing on that snow toy and don't be showing off," she admonished her husband lovingly. "I don't want to be scraping you out of some snowbank." She paused. "Madison? We're here for you, honey. You be careful up there in that airplane. I'll swan, you just amaze the heck out of me. I'll put the coffee on and cook up a pot of soup. You all will need something hot when you get back. Over and out for now."

A sheen of tears blurred Maddie's eyes for a moment. Their neighbors had dropped everything to form a search party. This was a fine community, one she wanted to bring her daughter up in—and the future children she would have.

Silence stretched in seconds, broken only by the drone of the Cessna's engine and the voices on the two-way radio as the search party alternately called Brice's name and gave their coordinates.

She banked the airplane slowly, the ground sliding beneath her in a field of blinding white fragmented by the occasional stand of naked cottonwoods, a pretty good indication that a creek was nearby, though it was hard to tell with all the snow-drifts. She kept an eye on the compass and tried to visually record landmarks in her memory. In the vast openness, it would be easy to lose her bearings.

Her hand covered her stomach, and she sent up a silent prayer that they'd find Brice in time.

BRICE OPENED HIS EYES slowly, taking a careful inventory of his surroundings, and of the aches and pains that were making themselves known all over his body.

His boot was caught in the vee of a rotted cottonwood. He tried to pull his foot from the boot, but the ankle was wedged too tightly, effectively trapping him. There were snow-covered rocks beneath him, and a steep wall of white around him.

His prison.

It was freezing, yet he felt sweat slide down his temples and beneath his arms, felt himself on the verge of panic. If the snow above him gave way, he'd be buried.

It was his worst nightmare—bringing back all the memories. Once again he was five years old, trapped. He'd been cold and wet then, too. So scared. Screaming until he was hoarse. And nobody came. Nobody knew he was missing. Dad thought Mom was watching him, but Mom had already packed up and left, not even bothering to tell Kyle and Brice goodbye.

He shook the memories away. He was too old to be watched after now. He was a tough rancher. A man.

But like all those years ago, it would be a long time before someone thought to look for him. His own men would assume he'd be fine on his own—an impression he himself had fostered.

MADDIE THOUGHT she saw something—just a flash from the corner of her eye. She put the plane into a tight circle, the wingtip pointing down, and felt as though the g-forces were rearranging her brain matter. She fought the wooziness in her stomach, willed herself to concentrate. She had to fly the plane and search at the same time. This was new to her.

She caught sight of the movement and her spirits fell. It was only a deer.

Frustration and fear tightened her stomach. Above her was gray sky. Below was stark white, so beautiful, so unstable. They were running out of time, literally. Running before a storm. "Where are you, Brice?"

She keyed the mike. "Brice? This is Maddie. Talk to me... please."

AT THE SOUND of her voice, Brice's heart leaped. He swore and tugged frantically at the boot wedged in the tree. He could hear the tremble in Madison's voice, pictured her at the house by the two-way radio. In his tumble into the ravine, his own portable unit had come unclipped from his belt and lay six feet out of reach.

He stretched out his arm, shifted his body. But the tree held him prisoner. The drifts were piled high on either side of him. No one would see him.

He gave a sharp two-toned whistle, a signal that would send Samson back to the barn. The horse had uncanny instincts for finding his way. He would leave tracks that would lead here. Plus, he was damned worried about his horse standing around, a perfect prey for the wolves.

He heard Samson blow and paw the ground. More snow and rocks fell around him. Wiping the freezing snow off his face, he whistled again. "Go, Samson!"

Well trained, the horse obeyed. Brice strained his ears, listening to the jingle of Samson's bridle, the clop of his hooves against snow.

Soon all was silent again. And Brice was truly alone. Just as he'd predicted he would be.

The wind whistled overhead. He stared at the snow crowding him. The least little thing could trigger a slide—a slide that would bury him alive.

He lost all sense of time as he stared at the blinding white. To keep the fear from running away with him, he pictured Madison's face; the way she laughed at her mistakes; the way she trudged ahead, anyway; the way her blue eyes darkened in the heat of passion….

Caught up in his imagery, it was a minute before his brain registered the sound. The buzz of a small airplane. Flying low. Who would fly low like that? He hadn't been gone long enough for Search and Rescue to form a team.

And he was the only rancher around for miles who had a plane—and a pilot's license.

The sound came closer, and his heart pounded. They'd never see him down here. Adrenaline pumped as he tried to focus on his options. His rifle and two-way radio were out of reach. His hat was buried beneath a layer of snow. He needed a flare of some kind, something that could be seen from the sky.

Using his teeth, he pulled off his glove, then untied his bandanna, his fingers stiff from cold. Picking up an icy rock, he wrapped the red cotton around the stone and retied the knot, listening to the drone of the engine, louder now. He timed the sound…closer, closer. The timing was so important.

Please, God, let the pilot be looking down. He counted to three, lifted his shoulder from the ground, and hurled the rock, wincing at the pain in his shoulder.

The bandanna sailed like a startled robin over the top of the snow bank, out of sight.

The Cessna flew so close…so damned close. He caught a flash of blue on the wingtip.

*Come on, come on! Bank to the right—a little more...
please!*

He yelled, even though he knew the pilot couldn't hear him.
And just like all those years ago when he'd been a boy, trapped
in a dark, cold well, his throat ached from the effort.

He couldn't see where the bandanna had landed, didn't know
if the weight of the rock had buried his makeshift flare, or if
the pilot would even look down.

If he'd just thrown it a little harder, a little higher, it would
have darn near hit the plane. Adrenaline pumping, frustration
roiling, he jerked at his trapped boot, kicking at the unforgiving
wood with his free foot, struggling like a wild animal caught
in barbwire.

The pitch of the engine changed, banking...going farther
away instead of closer.

"No, damn it!" Defeated, he dropped his head back to the
cold ground, battling the panic over the walls of white closing
in on him.

His one opportunity and he'd blown it.

Just like he'd blown so many things in his life.

Chapter Fifteen

Maddie shivered, nerves screaming. She was damned rusty at this flying business—at least this kind, where she was so close to the ground and performing tight turns. Beneath her was a carpet of white so blinding it made her eyes water. She hadn't thought to grab sunglasses.

She could see the road in the distance, saw Dan and Mike's truck, pacing her. Thick clouds were moving in lower. She wouldn't be able to scud-run this close to the ground much longer. More snow would fall soon. Very soon. *Oh, God, please!*

To the right of the plane, she saw a set of tracks. Squinting, she could just make out a riderless horse as it appeared from a valley and crested the hill.

She stabbed the mike button. "Dan! I think I see Samson!" She looked at the compass, then at the road, trying to get her bearings. "I'm flying due south. The highway's to my left—east. I'm just passing over a mining shack."

"I see you. I know the shack."

"Okay, I'm going in for a tighter circle." Darn it, she'd thought those tracks were from the deer. Had they been from Brice's horse? She followed the trail, heart pounding, palms sweating. Her grip on the yoke was so tight it was a wonder the plane was even flying straight.

She keyed the mike on the radio. "Brice? Can you hear me?

It's Maddie. Come in." No answer. She felt tears sting her eyes, but battled them back. This was no time to fall apart. Either he couldn't answer—a scenario she didn't want to dwell on—or he'd lost his radio.

In her mind she pictured him as she'd last seen him, wearing his standard jeans with buckskin chaps buckled around his thighs, a blue-and-black-plaid flannel shirt, a red paisley bandanna tied around his neck, a heavy jacket and his black hat.

Eyes straining, she searched for a speck of color among all the white.

She almost missed it, just a dot of red, like a tiny marker flag in the snowdrift.

Her hands cramped from the death grip she kept on the yoke, and she prayed like mad that she wouldn't stall out and end up diving nose first into the ground. The blinding white messed with her depth perception, gave her a dizzying sense of vertigo.

Not now, she screamed silently. She blinked, concentrating, hating to take her eyes off the ground, yet knowing she needed to monitor the gauges.

In her peripheral vision, she saw Randy coming from the north, trailing Brice's horse behind him. Below her were tree roots sticking out of the earth. It almost looked as though the Cessna's wingtip was going to clip the ground.

Fighting the nerves, trusting her instincts as a pilot, she held the tight turn, ignoring the stall light and screaming alarm.

What had appeared to be flat ground was actually a snowdrift that formed an inverted vee in the landscape. A ravine hidden by the snow bank.

And Brice.

Oh, hold on!

She keyed the mike. "I found him! He's in what looks like a dried-up creek bed. Do you guys see me? Can you make it out here?"

"Can do," Dan replied.

"I'm headed your way," Randy said.

She was so caught up in looking at Brice, she hadn't realized she'd lost altitude and the Cessna was in imminent danger of shearing off a treetop. She slammed the throttle to full power and jerked back on the yoke, pulling up and out of the turn, her heart pounding so hard she thought she might throw up. Taking a breath, calmer now that she'd found him, she went in for another tight circle.

She could see his expression—horrified and irritated. She laughed, sure he was wondering what kind of maniac was flying his plane and darn near crashing it.

Then she sobered when she noticed his struggle. She pressed the mike button. "It looks like a tree is trapping his leg. Dan, can you call Doc Adams on the cellular?"

"This here's Moe at base. I'll make that call." A pause. "You done real good, missy." The old cowboy's voice was soft and gruff and full of emotion.

Three minutes later the ground rescue arrived at the site. Dan and Mike hopped out of the truck armed with ropes.

"Careful of the edge!" Maddie warned. "It looks like it could give any minute now."

Dan waved his hat in acknowledgment. Maddie banked for another tight circle, the g-forces making her light-headed, making the blood rush to her head and her stomach churn like an unsteady whirlpool.

She hardly noticed the discomfort because her excitement and relief was so enormous.

Good heavens, what had happened to her nice, staid, sensible life? The one she'd planned right down to the minute?

Love. That's what had happened.

When this was over and done with, when Brice was safely back home, they were going to quit pussyfooting around. She intended to stay, and he would darn well have to get used to it!

BRICE WATCHED the Cessna angle into another turn. By God he'd lost a good ten years off his life when the wing had nearly clipped those trees.

Especially now that he realized it was Madison flying his plane. When the heck had she learned to fly? She was so low he could see her blond hair, her round spectacles.

She'd found him. Come looking for him. Rescued him before he'd been buried in a frozen grave.

Emotion formed an aching lump in his throat. She was an amazing woman. These weren't the actions of a city girl. Dear God, she fit into his world so perfectly. He couldn't imagine having to live without her. Knew that he'd do anything to get her to stay.

He heard the slam of a truck door, the pounding of horses hooves.

"Boss? You okay?"

The sound of the ex-rodeo rider's voice was like sweet music. "Yeah, Dan. Just pissed. Damned tree's wrapped around my boot tighter than a bear trap."

"We'll have you out in a jiff. Just sit tight. Gotta go slow so we don't knock this snow down on you."

Brice didn't have much choice other than to sit tight. But he hated being in this position, unable to control his own destiny. The drone of the Cessna overhead snagged his attention again. The sky was getting darker.

"I've lost my two-way, Dan. I assume you're in contact with that Cessna up there?"

Dan's smiling face appeared over the snowdrift. On his belly, he slowly lowered a rope. "That's Madison flying your plane. Hell of a pilot. Hell of a woman." There was awe in Dan's voice.

Brice felt that awe, and more. He had to clear his throat before he could speak. "Yeah, she is that. You tell her to hightail it back and get that plane on the ground while she can still see. These clouds could close in, any minute now."

"Sure thing, boss. Maddie?"

"I'm here, Dan. Is he all right?"

"Boss says everything's A-okay. Says you better land before you get caught in bad weather."

"Roger, Dan."

Brice stared at his portable radio that was just out of reach, the sound of Madison's voice making his heart beat faster.

"Uh, Dan? Tell Brice..."

Her voice trailed off. *What? Tell me what?*

"Never mind," she said. Brice swore, wishing like hell he could reach the radio, demand that she finish what she was about to say.

The bump on his head must have done more damage than he'd thought—scrambling his brains, making him read more into her tone than was likely there, making him hope.

Because for just a moment he'd imagined that she was about to declare her undying, everlasting love.

Yeah, his brain was scrambled all right. Women didn't offer him everlasting anything.

Then again, most women weren't like Madison.

My God, she'd flown his plane!

He listened to the Cessna's engine as it got farther and farther away, then closed his eyes and waited for his men to get down the embankment and free his trapped boot.

MADDIE WAS IN THE KITCHEN with Letty, Doc, Nancy Adams and Moe, who still had Abbe cradled against his chest, fighting off the women, refusing to hand the baby over.

When she heard the truck pull into the yard, her heart lurched, and she had an unreasonable urge to brush her hair, to take off these glasses and put in her contact lenses, to put on a little makeup, spritz on more perfume.

The back door swung open before she could make up her mind one way or the other.

His expression looked darker than a thundercloud, and his disposition was about as surly as a bear with a splinter in his paw.

Masculine intent radiated from him as he stalked across the room, never acknowledging the neighbors who were there, never even glancing at the men who trailed him through the door. He stopped right in front of her, his chest nearly brushing her breasts.

"What the hell were you thinking?"

"Excuse me?" She tilted her head back to get a good look at him. He was six feet five inches of righteous indignation. What in the world was his problem? This certainly wasn't the grateful homecoming she'd expected.

"You could have been caught in a storm, crashed the plane."

Her eyes widened, and she imagined she looked like a startled owl behind the magnified lenses of her glasses. The urge to punch him was powerful. She managed to subdue it. Barely.

"I freeze my butt off out looking for you, and all you're worried about is your plane?"

"No, damn it! I was worried about you!" He was shouting, and before she could point out that fact to him and shout right back, he grabbed her by the shoulders, jerked her against him and covered her open, astonished mouth with his.

She'd never been kissed like this before, and was certain she wasn't the sort of woman who normally inspired such aggression, such spontaneity. The power of the kiss whipped through her, the danger of it thrilling her. It was a kiss filled with frustration, and fear…and something else. Something that felt gentle, caring, something that felt a lot like love.

They were both breathing heavily by the time he released her mouth. His gaze, however, remained locked with hers.

Stunned, she couldn't look away.

Someone discreetly cleared their throat. A pot clanged against the stove. Abbe squealed, happily testing her lungs.

Their kitchen was full of people, and they were acting like two fierce, hungry animals—right in front of God and everybody.

Maddie smoothed her hair, flipped it behind her ear and shoved her glasses back in place. She cleared her throat.

"Well. We should probably have Doc take a look at your foot."

"My foot's fine." He still sounded as though he were a breath away from losing his cool.

Had she done that to him? Did he actually care that much? "Why don't we let Doc be the judge of that? I saw you limping when you came in."

He didn't move, just watched her with an intensity that made her squirm. "Where'd you learn to fly like that?"

A soft laugh burst out. "I didn't know I knew how to fly like *that*. I usually try to keep the altitude a bit higher, and I definitely make it a point to go in a fairly straight line. And I don't even want to think about all the FAA rules I broke skimming along the treetops like that."

The corner of his lips twitched, and the turmoil in his eyes eased into amused admiration. "Emergencies are an exception."

"Oh, I'm glad to know that." They really shouldn't be looking at each other like this, with a roomful of people watching.

Doc broke the tension. "Best get over here and let me have a gander at that foot."

WITH ALL THE COMMOTION of the neighbors in the house, it was evening before they had a chance to talk again. Oddly enough, it seemed to Maddie as though Brice had been deliberately avoiding her after that heated kiss.

The house was silent as a tomb now that everyone had gone, but he still hadn't come to her.

She went to check on Abbe and stopped short in the doorway.

The room was lit only by the soft glow of a lamp shaped like a lamb. Brice stood by the crib, cradling the sleeping baby in his arms. The sight brought tears to her eyes. She wanted permanence, a family to call her own. She wanted this man.

She'd come here under false pretenses, on the run, and turned his life upside down, saddled him with an unwanted wife and baby—not to mention the damage he'd done to his credit cards with all the baby stuff he'd ordered.

And her microwave.

And the jeans he'd discreetly replaced when she'd ruined his others.

All her life she'd been surrounded by people, yet she'd been a loner really. And now that she'd allowed herself to open up to others, to trust, she was all the more determined not to lose what she'd come to love: this small community in Wyoming; all the great people; Moe Bertelli...

Brice DeWitt.

He was one of a kind. The type of man she'd always dreamed of but had never thought she would find. The type of man who had staying power, who would stick around for the long haul—unlike her father, who she now realized she'd been using as a yardstick with which to measure every other relationship.

She'd made a decision up in the plane, that when this was all over, they were going to quit pussyfooting around. To hell with pride. Maybe he didn't love her now, but there was no reason why those feelings couldn't grow. And if not, she had enough for both of them. There would be no more talk of an annulment, no more of this three-month-trial business.

If she had to, she would beg. She wanted this man—on any terms. Wanted whatever he would give her.

Then she heard him speak softly to the baby, and her heart lodged in her throat.

"I don't know what to do, princess. I'm not good with fancy words, and I don't trust a lot of folks to stick around. It can get kind of lonely out here, but it's my life. And I thought that life was pretty well mapped out until you and your mama landed on my doorstep. From the first moment I held you in my hands, I fell in love. I didn't want to, but there it is. And I surely didn't want to fall in love with your mother...but, well, there that is, too. I swear I was a gonner from the minute I opened the front door and found her standing there, shivering, wearing that fussy coat with the fur on the hood."

Maddie covered her trembling lips with her fingers, trying to hold in the emotion. She couldn't do it, and words burst from her lips.

"Why the heck didn't you say that in the first place!"

He whirled around. "You scared me half to death, and I almost dropped the baby."

"You'd never drop her."

For a long moment he just stared at her, his gaze traveling from her head to her toes, as though she were his heart's desire, as though he couldn't get enough of the sight of her.

Then he turned and gently laid Abbe back in the crib, covering her with a blanket, his fingers lingering on her soft cheek.

He moved toward Maddie, reached out and gently touched her cheek, much the same way he'd just done with the baby, the gesture so reverent, so achingly soft.

Shadows played over his high cheekbones, accenting the hollows in his cheeks and the hint of dark stubble around his jaw. His shoulders were so broad, his hands so strong and capable, hands that could subdue a terrorized cow or gently cradle a baby. Hands that could map a woman's body, make her feel cherished and wild at the same time.

"Let's get out of here so we don't wake the baby."

She nodded and walked by his side to the living room.

Brice tossed another log onto the fire, watching as sparks showered and sucked up the flue. His heart was pounding and his throat felt as though it was closing up. Out of habit he started to open the window, then realized he didn't need that anymore. The closed-in feelings were gone; the panic that he'd always been holding at bay had disappeared.

In its place was a different sort of panic. What if Madison didn't return his feelings? Or what if she did, but she couldn't stay, couldn't handle the life-style?

Firelight reflected off her round glasses. Her hair shone like a yellow ray of sunshine.

Sunshine.

That's what she'd brought into his life.

"Did I thank you for saving my life?"

A small dimple creased her cheek when she smiled. God, why hadn't he noticed that before? He wanted a lifetime to learn about her, to not miss a single detail.

"Well, you were pretty busy hollering at me for taking your plane."

"I ought to be ashamed."

Her blond brows were raised above her glasses in that spunky way that made him want to grab her and kiss her and never let go.

"Thank you, sunshine."

"Actually, you rescued me by delivering my baby, and I'm happy that I could return the favor."

He saw her twisting the wedding band on her finger. Just that simple gesture had adrenaline pumping his heart into a frenzy, and he was across the room in three strides, his hands gripping her shoulders.

"Damn it, I don't want gratitude, and I don't want a score card of favors to return."

In contrast to his outburst, her words were nearly a whisper. "What do you want, Brice?"

He dropped his hands, took a step back. "I want you to stay." They were the hardest words he'd ever said. His voice was sandpaper rough, filled with stark emotion he didn't even try to hide.

"For how long?"

"For as long as you want."

"Why?" she asked softly.

He frowned. Here he stood with his heart in his hands and his pride on the floor and she asked him why? "What do you mean?"

She eased closer, her blue eyes earnest as she stared up at

him. "Exactly what I said. It's a very simple question, Brice. Why do you want me to stay?"

"Because you're important to me."

"And?"

"And what?"

"Is that all?"

He made a frustrated sound deep in his throat. "No. I want you to stay because I love you, damn it!"

She blinked. And then she laughed. "Well. I don't think I ever pictured a man shouting his feelings quite like this."

He stared at her as though appalled that she could laugh at such a time. Then his expression cleared and the corners of his mouth twitched. "Woman, you're driving me crazy."

She smiled, liking the fact that she made him nuts. That was a good thing. "So, why haven't you said so before? That you love me, I mean."

"I've been trying to tell you for the past few weeks. But I didn't want to put pressure on you by coming right out and saying it."

She put her palm on his chest, right over his heart. "I'm a practical woman, Brice DeWitt—a Wyoming ranch woman— and I'd just as soon have the words."

He covered her hand with his, drew her closer.

"You know, it seems to me I haven't exactly heard any confessions of undying love coming from you."

"Ah, but I've been saying it for the past three months. With my body. And my touch. Haven't you heard me?"

"Touché." Softly, reverently, he lowered his head, kissing her in a way that made her go up on her toes, lean into him.

"I love you, sunshine. Be my wife."

"I already am." The words were muffled against his mouth.

He pulled back just a bit, looked down at her. Love was shining in his deep blue eyes, yet there was still a shadow of reserve. She wanted to banish that reserve, but he spoke before she could.

"I mean for real, and forever. I don't want a temporary marriage. I want you and Abbe to be my family, to fill my heart and my days. I promise I'll make you happy. And if the winters get too much for you, we'll take off somewhere, go be snowbirds in Florida, or California—"

She stopped his words with her fingers pressed to his mouth. "We don't need to be snowbirds. Anywhere you are is where I want to be, whether it's in snow or sunshine. I'll be your wife."

He whooped and lifted her right off the ground, twirling her in a circle.

"Besides," she added when her head stopped spinning, "it just wouldn't seem right to get an annulment when you're going to be a daddy."

He lowered her feet to the ground, held her close, his chin resting atop her head.

"I'm already a daddy. I brought Abbe into this world and she's mine. I love her, just like I love you." His lips seduced her as his hands traveled beneath her sweater. "And right now I think we both have on too many clothes."

Maddie's heart was full. She smiled against his lips, moved with him as he walked her backward toward the sofa.

"Brice?"

"Hmm?"

"In a roundabout way, I was working up to telling you something."

"Mmm. Later."

"Okay. I suppose it can wait to tell you that I'm not allergic to you."

He stopped, went absolutely still, looked down at her, confusion and cautious hope in his eyes. "Maybe you better tell me now."

"Evidently our body chemistries are a perfect match."

"What's that supposed to mean?"

"It means I'm going to have your baby."

"That's not—"

She placed her fingers over his mouth, stopping his words. "Possible? Think again, cowboy. The newest addition to the DeWitt family should arrive in about seven months' time."

"But…"

"When Sharon told you she was allergic to you, that didn't mean you couldn't father a child. It just meant that it couldn't happen with *her*."

"Oh, God, sunshine. Are you sure?"

She nodded. "Nancy confirmed it last week. Seems you're destined to have unexpected babies drop into your life."

Brice didn't know how to contain his emotions. My God, how had he gotten so lucky? He stared down at Madison, his wife, the mother of his children. *His children!* It sounded so good. His chest felt so full.

"Abbe was enough for me," he said, awed.

"I know. But you always said you wanted family. I figured that two or three more babies would be okay with you."

He snatched her to him, held her tight against his chest. "It's okay…" He swallowed, cleared his throat. "Yeah, more babies is really okay." He cupped her cheeks, held her gaze, his love so huge he was sure it would somehow burst out of him. This woman simply filled his soul when he'd thought it would be empty forever.

And he thanked God she'd dropped into his life.

"Today, when I was down in that ravine, all I could think about was that this would be just like the last time. That nobody would bother to look for me. That no one would care. But you came."

"Of course I came. You rescued me, Brice—and not just by delivering Abbe. You took away the loneliness when I didn't even know I was lonely…"

"And?"

"And I rescued you right back," she said softly. "Because I love you."

He kissed her long and deep. She could hardly draw a breath when he raised his head.

"You're sure it's not too soon to have another baby?"

"No. It's not. I'm fine."

There was a gleam in his eye. "We'll have to outfit another nursery. What do you think of bears this time? Seems to be a popular theme in the catalogues."

She laughed. "As your accountant, I'm going to have to talk to you about the way you use that credit card."

"Mmm. Let's talk later. Right now your accounting talents are the farthest thing from my mind.

* * * * *